A TOTAL TEARDOWN

THE BUILDERS, BOOK 4

VANESSA GRAY BARTAL

DRY CREEK PRESS

PROLOGUE

Jessamine Samperi stood in a huddled mass of friends, trying to simultaneously blend in and stand out. Freshman homecoming marked not only her first high school dance but the first time she had been let loose to go out alone with her friends. Of course her saintly older brother Benedict was also in attendance, but he was sitting at a table across the room, laughing hard at something his friend, Lou, was saying. Her older brothers were protective. She had been afraid Benny might hover all night, but he had seemed happy to deposit her at the door and find Lou.

Now it was as if she truly was alone, and she couldn't help but relish in her freedom a little. With so many Samperis, alone time came at a premium.

"Look at Everett," Jessamine's friend, Laura, said. "He's so hot." Everett Rains was their school's "it" guy—handsome, popular, and quarterback of the football team. A junior, he had stolen the heart of nearly every freshman girl, and most of the sophomores and juniors, too.

"Jess doesn't think so," Carolyn said, and all the girls turned to look at her.

"He's come over to the house a few times to hang out with Benny. It sort of takes the shine off when you see a guy get in a belching contest with your brothers."

"Jess thinks everyone is beneath her," Ashley accused. Jessamine didn't like her much. In fact there were only a couple of girls in her group of friends she actually enjoyed. The rest seemed too bent on attaining popularity at all costs, even if it meant stepping on people to get there. Jessamine didn't like to be mean to people, and with her brother, Benny, always on watch, she didn't have much opportunity to be cruel, even if she wanted to.

"That's not true," Carolyn said with a coy look to Jess.

"What? You like someone? Who is it?" Laura asked.

"Carolyn," Jessamine intoned.

"I didn't say who," Carolyn replied.

"Who is it? You have to tell us," Laura demanded.

"Why do I have to tell you?" Jessamine asked.

"Because it's the law," Ashley said.

"Come on, Jess, you've never liked anyone before. This is a big deal. Maybe we could help you," Laura suggested.

"Uh, no, you definitely could not. He is totally not into me," Jess said.

"How do you know?" Laura asked.

"Carolyn, tell them he's not into me," Jessamine demanded.

"I don't know, Jess. He might be, if he knew you existed," Carolyn said, laughing.

Jessamine rolled her eyes. There was no way anyone could be into her. As far as she was concerned, she was a big-haired, big-nosed freak. Her too-large nose bothered her so much she had asked her parents for plastic surgery for Christmas, forcing her father into a stream of such rapid Italian that Jessamine, who was fairly fluent, hadn't been able to understand what he was saying.

Your father says no, her mother had said at the end of the long rant.

"Tell us," the girls began to chant.

"Come on, Jess. You owe us this," Ashley said.

"Why do I owe you?" Jessamine asked.

"Because it's part of the code of friendship. You tell your girls who you like. It's the way it is, and if you don't tell, then you can't be part of us."

"Ash," Carolyn chided.

"No, I'm sick of it, Carolyn. She never comes to any of our stuff," Ashley said.

"That's because my parents are strict, and I have to work," Jessamine said. On her fourteenth birthday, her father had included her in the family business and started teaching her the ropes. Though she would never admit it to her friends, she preferred construction to mindless hanging out and girl drama any day. Being on the job was the first time her older brothers had treated her as an equal, and she was good at everything her father had taught her, at least so far. It felt like being a real grownup. Then she had to return to school and have conversations like these, about who likes whom and who is friends with whom. Suddenly the next three years of high school loomed before her like a long, dusty road.

The more she thought about it, the less she cared if the other girls knew who she liked. This wasn't her real life, she suddenly realized. Real life was her family and her work. They were her future. Someday high school would merely be a distant, uncomfortable memory.

"Fine, I like Milo," Jessamine announced to the surprise of everyone but Carolyn.

"But he's so…bad," Laura said.

"Jess thinks he's misunderstood," Carolyn added.

Jessamine didn't say anything, but it was true. Milo Eliopoulos, a senior, had first caught her attention because he was the only other kid in their school with an ethnic-sounding name. Everyone else was a Smith, Jones, Harris, or something equally WASP-ish. They shared a study hall, and she had noted him one day, wondering if his Greek family was as crazy as her Italian family. He had been reading a book, *The Catcher in the Rye.* Until then the only boy she had seen read for pleasure was her little brother, Giovanni, who always had his nose in a book.

As she stared at Milo, while he stared at the book, she began to have the uncomfortable realization that he was incredibly nice look-ing. His dark hair flopped rakishly over deep blue eyes, and he had a dimple on his right cheek. But he was a total delinquent, wasn't he? He had a reputation as such and was often in detention, but Jess had her doubts. He *was* often in detention, namely for talking back to teachers, but teachers seemed to love him regardless. He smoked, drank, partied, skipped school, and was generally up for any sort of mischief, but was he really *bad*? What made someone bad? For the first time, Jess's black and white rules of wrong and right began to come under scrutiny. Did flouting school rules make one bad, or was it personal character?

She had watched once as a kid in the hallway dropped a five-dollar bill. Milo retrieved it and handed it back to him. Of course he stuffed it down the kid's pants and gave him a wedgie, but he had generally done the right thing, hadn't he? And there were other signs. One time he stood up for a girl in Jess's class who had spent middle school trying to stop having bathroom accidents. Everyone was calling her Pee-pee Pants McGee and Milo had put a stop to it. And once she saw him help the school secretary after she slipped on ice. He had pulled her up and held onto her all the way into the building, holding the door for her when they reached it. Didn't all those little acts of kind-ness mean he was, in fact, a good guy?

"Look, there he is," Laura hissed and Jessamine whirled to look. Milo stood lounging in the doorway, looking cool and unruffled in a t-shirt and jeans.

"We're supposed to dress up," Ashley said, affronted by his casual attire.

"He does look good," Carolyn admitted.

Milo scanned the room, his gaze pausing on the group of freshman girls who were staring at him. He gave them a half smile that made his dimple appear.

"Okay, yeah, I'm beginning to see the appeal," Laura said, her tone a little unsteady. "You should totally ask him to dance, Jess."

"What?" Jessamine exclaimed. "No way. You guys, no way. He's a *senior*. He doesn't even know I exist."

"So? Make him realize you're alive. And none of his pothead friends are here yet. You should nab him before they get here. Guys are always easier to approach when they're alone," Carolyn said.

Jessamine shook her head.

"Fine, then I'll do it," Ashley said, flouncing her long, luxurious hair. "I'll ask him to dance."

Not for the first time, Jessamine wanted to punch her. She didn't want Milo; she only wanted to take him because Jessamine liked him. And Ashley had the kind of far advanced raw sensuality that belied her fourteen years. Guys flocked to her, even guys like Milo who appeared immune.

"I'll do it," she said, surprising everyone, including herself.

"Go, Jess," Carolyn said.

"I'll believe it when I see it," Ashley said.

Ignoring her, Jessamine pushed her hair back, straightened her shoulders, and made the long walk across the gym toward Milo who watched her approach with something like surprised amusement.

"May I help you?" he asked when she finally reached him.

"I was, um, wondering if maybe you wanted to dance," she said.

He regarded her for a few seconds in heavy silence—while Jessamine hung in the balance, feeling as if she might throw up on his shoes—"Sure, why not?" he finally agreed. Then he did the unthinkable by clasping her hand and leading her onto the dance floor.

"What's your name?" he asked.

"Jessamine," she said, purposely not telling him she was a Samperi. If he knew Benny or Joe, he might run away, scared to touch her.

"You look like a good girl, Jessamine."

"I am," she said, not having any idea how to pretend to be anything else.

He smiled and Jessamine thought her heart might explode. "Have you ever danced with a guy before?"

"Do cousins count?" she asked.

"Cousins never count," he said. He picked up her arms and put them around his neck before resting his hands on her waist.

"Now what?" she asked.

"Now we dance," he said, and they began gently swaying to a slow song.

"It's kind of boring," Jessamine said after a while.

"Things are never as exciting as you think they'll be," he said.

"Senior wisdom," she commented.

He chuckled. "I guess so."

"What else can you tell me? I have three years left here," she said.

The song came to an end, and he stopped dancing. "Stop looking for trouble, or it will definitely find you." He touched his finger to the tip of her nose before letting her go and walking away.

Jessamine made the long walk back to her friends with wobbly legs. Had she really done that or had it been a dream? Either way, it was perfect and she never wanted to wake up.

"That was amazing," Carolyn said, grabbing her hand and giving it a squeeze. "What did he say to you?"

"I don't even know," Jessamine said. She felt dazed. The rest of the dance went on without her, and she didn't care. She stood still, reliving the memories. She had been brave, and it had paid off. Milo had danced with her, smiled at her, *touched her nose*. Suddenly she felt the need for more adventure.

"I'm going to go find him again," she whispered to Carolyn.

"What are you going to do?" Carolyn whispered back. Ashley and Laura were busy talking to some guys, and Jessamine was glad for the cover. She didn't want them to know what she was up to.

"I don't know. Maybe I could get him to kiss me."

Carolyn put her hand over her mouth and nodded enthusiastically. Jessamine took a bracing breath and sneaked away before Laura or Ashley could notice her. Surreptitiously, she had been tracking Milo's movements so she knew he was now outside with his friends. It was possible he had left, but she didn't think so. His usual method was to hang out on the fringes of every gathering, making fun of everything with his friends. With a glance at her brother, Benny, to make sure he wasn't watching her, she opened the door and slipped outside.

As she had thought, Milo was with a group of his friends, smoking. She sneaked closer in the darkness, hugging the building for support.

"Hey, Milo, did you get paid for the babysitting job?" one of his friends asked.

Milo babysits? Jessamine wondered, and then realized they were talking about her.

"Dude, dancing with a freshman. Is that where we're at now?" another of his friends asked.

"She asked. What was I going to do, break her heart forever?" Milo said. "You have to be sensitive about these things."

Another friend laughed. "Right, that's you, Mr. Sensitive."

Jessamine's heart melted a little until Milo continued. "Besides, have you seen the nose on that thing? I'm clearly the only action she was going to get tonight. Sometimes you have to toss the dogs a bone."

His friends laughed and laughed while Jessamine's heart broke into a million tiny pieces. Unobserved, she slipped back into the building, went to the bathroom, and cried until her tears ran dry.

CHAPTER 1

*H*e did not want a woman, nor any of the trouble having a woman might bring. But when he saw her sitting at the bar, he couldn't seem to stop his feet from making an approach, and then his lips were moving and he was saying things.

"Hey."

The woman turned to look at him, giving him the full blast of her stunning good looks. She was tall with long, long legs. Her hair was big and long and dark and curly and her face was even more spectacular than the rest of her. Her skin was olive-toned, her eyes an arresting mixture of green and copper, fringed by ridiculously long lashes, and her mouth—oh, the mouth. It was wide and expressive, especially now as her lip curled at the sight of him.

"Hey," she said, the word clipped and angry as if he had already done something to offend her. She turned back to her phone and continued texting.

Undeterred, he hopped onto the stool next to her. "What's your name?"

"You can call me, 'I don't talk to strange men in bars.'"

"Kind of wordy. Do you have a nickname?" he asked.

"Get lost," she said, still not looking up from the phone.

"Question: if you don't talk to men in bars, what are you doing in a bar?" he asked.

"Meeting someone."

"Hey, me too. What are the chances?" he said.

She didn't reply. He tried again.

"You look vaguely familiar."

She turned to him with the death glare again. "Really."

"Yes, like I've seen your face, but I can't think where," he said.

No response.

"Should we send out our wedding invitations now or wait until our first date?" he asked.

She fished in her bag, pulled out a container of pepper spray, and set it on the bar between them. Then returned to her phone.

"I can tell you meant that to be intimidating, but I'm a highly trained marine, so I have to tell you that a little pepper spray is meaningless to me," he said.

"Why don't we step outside? I can spray some directly in your eyeballs and you can show me all your elite training," she said, her eyes still glued to the phone.

"Are you a brain surgeon getting minute-by-minute updates on your phone?" he asked.

"Are you oblivious to any and all rejection?" she countered. "Or does the fact that I'm trying to work mean nothing to you?"

"It's almost nine on a Friday night. What kind of job do you do?" he asked. "And if you say it's illegal, know I will not automatically be turned off."

She blew out a breath and studiously ignored him.

"You're a tough nut," he noted.

"And you're clearly desperate, which makes you oh-so-much more attractive," she said.

"Congratulations, stranger lady. I don't think anyone has ever referred to me as desperate before," he said.

"Ugh," she groaned, rolling her eyes.

"See, that was incredibly expressive, but I'd prefer you to use your words."

She set down the phone and turned to face him. "I don't find you cute or charming or in any way interesting or intriguing. I am only here to meet friends for dinner, otherwise I would be working, as I am now trying to do while I wait. So take your conceited, self-involved, trying to be cute but ending up being pathetic self out of my space before I involve the bartender and ask to have you removed." She faced forward again and picked up the phone.

"*Wow,*" he mouthed. "Is this like a third-wave feminism thing? Do you hate all men or are you channeling a wicked witch of the west impression for personal reasons?"

"There's a wall," she said, waving her hand between them.

He pretended to knock on her imaginary wall. "Can I come over? I need to ask you a question."

She turned her back to him.

"I can still see you, and I bet you can still hear me," he said.

"Jess!" A new woman spoke from the bar's entrance, and the woman next to him, his woman, as he had already come to think of her, spun to look, her angry face transformed by a huge smile of welcome.

"Carolyn!" she exclaimed. She slid off the stood, rushed forward, and the two women hugged tightly. "I'm so, so, so sorry I couldn't make the rehearsal."

Carolyn waved her hand. "You've rehearsed one wedding, you've rehearsed them all. This is the most important part, and you made it. Everyone else should be here soon. David's parking the car."

She was joined by a man who scanned the room, his eyes settling on the man at the bar. "There he is." The two men greeted each other with a manly half-hug and then the two women turned to face the two men.

"Let me guess, he's in the wedding," Jessamine said as she surveyed the man who had been hitting on her at the bar.

"He's the best man," Carolyn's fiancé, David, said. "Milo Eliopoulos, meet Jessamine Samperi, the maid of honor."

"You're a Samperi. That's why you look familiar," Milo said. "I was between Joe and Benny. I didn't realize they had a sister."

"But you already…" Carolyn began, but Jessamine gave her a squeeze to stop the flow of words.

"Yes, I'm a Samperi. That's undoubtedly why you know me. Question: we're separating tonight, yes? Guys going their way, girls going ours?"

Milo drew in a sharp breath. "Ouch. I can't help but think that was directed at me."

"We're separating," Carolyn assured her. "From now on until tomorrow afternoon, I am a maiden, to be surrounded only by the support of other females." She stood on her toes and gave her fiancé a wholly inappropriate goodbye kiss while Jessamine and Milo stood awkwardly by.

"It seems like maybe we should get in on this, offer them some support so they're not so conspicuous," Milo said.

Jessamine blew a wayward strand of hair out of her eyes and crossed her arms.

"I'll take that as a maybe," Milo said. He gave her the smile, the one with the dimple, and Jessamine turned away.

When the kiss was over, Jessamine and Carolyn walked away toward the back room, arm in arm.

"What's up with the ice queen?" Milo asked David.

"Ice queen? Jess? She's one of the most fun, warmest people I know. Definitely my favorite of Carolyn's friends," David said.

"Did she go to our school, or was she cloistered?" he asked. There were four Samperi brothers. He couldn't imagine them letting a sister who looked like that get too far out of their sight.

"She was Carolyn's best friend. But, you know, they were three years behind us, so it's not like we would have hung out together," David said. He and Carolyn had met at work, years after high school was over. "Have you not seen her on TV?"

"TV?" Milo exclaimed.

"Wow, you really have been out of it. I forgot how much. The Samperis got a show on the home and garden channel, and it's been a huge hit. They've been everywhere, especially Jess. She's been on, like, every magazine and morning talk show for the last three months."

"That must be why she looks so familiar," Milo said, staring after her. "And why she's such a haughty, standoffish piece of work."

"This is my last night of freedom. Are we going to stand around and talk about women all night?" David asked.

"Twenty bucks says I can beat you at darts," Milo said.

"How about you just give me twenty bucks since you pathetically haven't hit a dartboard in a decade and I have to pay for a honeymoon to Aruba?" David replied.

"We'll see who's pathetic after tonight," Milo said. They turned and walked in the opposite direction from the ladies, and it took a lot of willpower for him not to turn and look over his shoulder for Jessamine Samperi.

CHAPTER 2

*J*essamine was exhausted. She had been on a nonstop shooting schedule, followed by the interview circuit. Yesterday she woke in New York City, did a stint on a morning show, spent the afternoon discussing the edits to her show at the home and garden channel's headquarters, stopped by Brooklyn to say hello to her Nonna, and miraculously made it back in time for Carolyn's bachelorette party. And now, on the first day off she'd had in months, it was Carolyn's wedding day. Jessamine was ecstatic for her friend, but a little melancholy, too. She was thirty-and-a-half years old, and Carolyn was the last of her single friends. Now who would she go out with, on the rare occasions she happened to get a day off? Her three closest friends, Vivian, Vivica, and Carolyn, were all gone and, even though marriage wasn't a death sentence, it felt like they all fell off a cliff. Even though Vivian married Jessamine's brother, Giovanni, it wasn't the same. They were a *couple.* As bad as it was to be the last of her friends still single, it was even worse to be the last one standing in her family. She never imagined her baby brother, Moss, five years her junior, would beat her to the altar, but his wedding was in a few weeks, and he already had a baby.

You don't want to get married, she reminded herself. She enjoyed her independence too much to settle down. If she wanted to knock out the wall in her kitchen and expand, she could, and she didn't need a man's approval to do so. In fact, she didn't even need a man's help to the renovation. She was incredibly self-sufficient, and she liked it that way. She was only feeling self-pity because she was drained and because Carolyn was the last of a dying breed, minus herself.

"I'm so sorry you got stuck with this job," Carolyn said. As maid of honor, Jessamine was the designated dress holder every time Carolyn had to use the bathroom. As bad luck would have it, she had a nervous bladder.

"Don't even worry about it," Jessamine said. "Besides, after tag teaming on the stomach flu our junior year, this seems like a walk in the park."

"But now you're all famous and stuff," Carolyn said.

"Gag, Carolyn, don't you ever, ever say that to me. And if I ever start to change and get too good to stand behind you holding your dress while you tinkle, please kill me."

"Deal," Carolyn said. "So, Milo Eliopoulos."

"Nope."

"Still not allowed to talk about it?" Carolyn said. Jessamine had refused to answer any questions about their encounter at the bar, no matter how much Carolyn prodded the night before.

"Nope. Suffice it to say we won't be having a round two on my teenage crush," Jessamine said.

"You never told me what happened at homecoming that night after you danced with him."

"Let's say I saw his true colors and had no desire for a repeat," Jessamine said.

"He's definitely gotten hotter," Carolyn said.

"How is this not talking about it? And why didn't you tell me he was David's best man?"

"Honestly? I totally forgot about the homecoming thing until I saw you guys together. It was so long ago, and then he graduated and you never mentioned him again. But then I saw the way he was looking at you last night, and it all came crashing back."

"Nope," Jessamine said.

"You're no fun," Carolyn said.

"I'm tons of fun. Now, you stand still while I lever you off the potty," Jessamine said, and Carolyn laughed.

"This is so embarrassing," she said.

"That's what weddings are for, an excruciating exercise in humiliation."

"Counting Vivica, this is your fourth wedding this year," Carolyn said.

"Don't I know it," Jessamine said. Her brother, Benny, had gotten married a mere three weeks before and Moss's wedding was still to come. "I'm becoming a wedding cake connoisseur, so it better not be dry. No pressure."

"If it's bad, are you going to blog about it?" Carolyn asked.

"Yes, in my free time I like to make fun of other people's weddings. It's my contribution to society."

"In all your vast free time," Carolyn said. "I feel like I haven't seen you in a year."

"I know, and I'm so sorry. It's been crazy since the show started," Jessamine said. "But I'm here, and I am totally present for whatever you need. So what do you need?"

Carolyn gave her an apologetic look.

"Again?" Jessamine said.

"After staying up all night, I drank a ton of coffee. Sorry."

"It's totally fine," Jessamine assured her. "By the way, if I ever get married, I'm planning to eat a lot of bad sushi so you can hold my hair while I puke. Fair warning."

"Turnabout is only fair," Carolyn said as they wedged her giant dress back into the stall.

At last it was time for Carolyn to walk down the aisle. Jessamine felt herself tearing up as she preceded her. David looked anxious and blissful, waiting for his bride. Benny had worn the same expression waiting for Lou, and soon Moss would wear the expression for Molly. It was, hands down, Jessamine's favorite part of any wedding.

Her eyes slid to the right and Milo, who wore what she deemed a mocking smile. Quickly, she trained her eyes forward again. It wouldn't do to become angry in this tender moment, and the sight of Milo made her enraged. It wasn't the insult from so long ago. Okay, it was. But she could tell that the interim had not improved him. He was cocky, and Jessamine loathed cocky men. Her brothers had their faults, but all of them were humble and hardworking. She lacked patience for anyone who wasn't the same.

She reached the end of the aisle and turned in time to see the flower girl, followed by Carolyn and her father, though she couldn't help but sneak a peek at David to catch his reaction. It didn't disappoint. David—who had once been a stoner in high school and miraculously turned into a solid and upstanding guy—was crying. And not just a little. Jessamine sniffled and made a concerted effort to push back the tears, so as not to ruin her mascara. Plus she had a job to do. Soon she would take Carolyn's heavy and magnificent bouquet and hold it through most of the service, and then there was the small flower girl to keep track of.

At last the vows were over, and it was time to walk back up the aisle. With Milo, the creep. He held out his arm to her and, to her surprise, didn't say a word. They posed for endless wedding pictures, and then it was time to go to the reception. The wedding party rode in a limousine and somehow Jessamine got stuck next to Milo.

"Well, well, well, Jessamine Samperi. We meet again."

"I've seen you the entire day," she said.

"I knew you were looking," he said. "You can no longer deny this heat between us."

"If you're feeling heat, you must have a fever. I'm stone cold," she said.

"I picked up on that last night. Lucky for you, I think it's all a veneer to cover your deep attraction to me," he said.

"You have not once asked if I'm married, engaged, or entangled. Why do you assume I'm single?" she asked.

"With a love like ours, it wouldn't matter if you were attached," he said.

"That's sick sentiment, but seems par for the course for you," she replied.

"Don't you want to know what my status is?" he asked.

"I'm dying to know. That's why I've asked so many, many times," she said.

"You probably asked Carolyn," he said.

"Really, really no," she said.

"I asked David about you because that's how much I care," he said.

"Wait, you mean you care enough to ask your close friend one simplifying question about me? It must be love," Jessamine said.

"David said you're famous, but I want you to know I loved you before I knew that. That's how you know my love is pure," he said.

"Do you read?" she blurted.

"I've been known to," he said. "Especially warning labels and grocery lists."

"No, I mean are you a dedicated reader, or was that part of your cool guy high school persona?" she asked.

"I read," he admitted, sounding uncharacteristically reticent. "What do you know about my high school persona?"

"We went to high school together," she informed him.

"You're admitting you noticed me in high school," he said.

"And you're admitting you didn't notice me at all," she said.

"You were younger. I didn't know a lot of freshman."

"I'd wager you had run-ins with a couple," she said.

"But not you. I would for sure remember you," he said.

"Do you think so?" she asked, tilting her head and leaning into him a little.

"What's happening? Was I granted magic wishes? Why are you suddenly not snapping my head off?"

"I'm giving you a chance to get a close-up of my face so you can make doubly certain you don't remember me from high school," she said. She crooked her finger at him. "Come closer. Take a good look."

He leaned in slightly until they were nose to nose. "To be honest, you're kind of blurry from this close up."

She gave him a light shove and leaned back.

"That was it? Did I pass the test?" he asked.

"I used to think you were the strong silent type. I miss those days," Jessamine said, squeezing the bridge of her nose.

"I think I know what this is about," he said.

She glanced up in surprise. "You do?"

"If you knew me in high school, you must be under the impression I'm trouble. But more than a decade in the marines has a way of straightening a man out. Turns out all I needed was some help growing up."

"You could not possibly be more wrong," she said. "For the record, I don't care if you're trouble. I don't care if you're a saint. In about two more hours, we will say goodbye forever, and I will forget all about you. I have never wanted time to go faster."

"Your brothers are nice. What happened to you?"

"I'm nice to nice people," she replied.

"I'm nice people," he said. "What have I ever done to you to make you believe otherwise?"

She gave him the death stare.

"For the record, I don't know what that means, but it's super sexy hot when you do it," he said.

"I don't like cocky men. I don't like flirts. I don't like men who pick up women in bars based on appearances. In short, I don't like you," she said.

"I'm beginning to think you don't like me," he said. "But I'm going to give it a little longer to make sure because, as the mother of my future children, I owe you that much."

"Congratulations, Milo, you've now surpassed my senior prom to make this the worst ride in a limo ever," she said.

"I'm going to take that as the compliment I know you meant it to be," Milo said. "Oh, look, we're here."

"Hallelujah, the nightmare is over," Jessamine said, but it turned out it was just getting started.

CHAPTER 3

Jessamine had to walk into the reception on Milo's arm. She tried to let go and mingle after that, but he followed her.

"Are you a puppy?" she asked, annoyed as she turned around and saw him tagging behind her.

"Do you want me to be?" he asked.

"Would it do any good to tell you how much you're getting on my nerves?" she asked.

"What do you think?" he replied, smiling.

"Why do I feel like if you weren't nice looking you'd probably be in prison right now?" she asked. It was clear people gave him a pass on his bad and annoying behavior because he was handsome, and that was another of Jessamine's pet peeves.

"That may be the most accurate summation of my life I've ever heard," he said, unconcerned.

She turned away from him and ran, almost literally, into her former friends Laura and Ashley. While her friendship with Carolyn had lingered and remained strong, everyone else from their high school group had faded away after graduation.

"Jess," Laura exclaimed, giving her a hug.

"Well, well, well," Ashley said, examining Milo with interest. "Don't tell me you actually bagged Milo."

"We are not together," Jessamine said. "Not even a little bit."

"So he's available?" Ashley said, offering up a come-hither smile that hadn't changed since she was in middle school, probably because it still worked the same. She was a beautiful woman, and she was highly cognizant of that fact.

"Absolutely, have at it. Milo, this is Ashley Taylor, another proud alumnus." She put her hand on his arm and drew him forward for the introduction.

Milo shook Ashley's hand, smiling his most charming and flirtatious smile. "So, Ashley Taylor, what can you tell me about Jessamine Samperi?"

"Probably not much since she's famous and above us mere mortals now," Ashley said, as catty as ever.

"Never change, Ashley," Jessamine said, smiling politely. "You two have a blast. I hope it ends in a marriage, for both your sakes."

She turned and made a quick escape, but in seconds Milo had caught up with her. "Why are you here?" she asked, exasperated.

"Because we're sitting at the same table, and I'm hungry," he said.

"Why did you leave Ashley so soon? She seemed really into you."

"No, she seemed really into beating you, there's a difference," he said.

"At least you're perceptive," she said.

"I'm going to take that as 'I love you, Milo,'" he said.

"You can't possibly be this desperate," she said.

"I'm not," he said and gave her the smile that made her traitorous heart do a little flip flop. He was an incredibly physically appealing man, drat him. But Jessamine had never been accused of being shallow. Looks were low on her comprehensive list of desired qualities. Faithfulness and loyalty were high, and she sensed he was lacking both.

"If I ask you an honest question, will you give me an honest answer?" she asked.

"Fire away," he said.

"When is the last time you cheated on someone?"

He squinted, thinking. "Fourteen years ago."

"How do I know you're not lying?" she asked.

"Are you not familiar with the marines? It's sort of against the code," he said.

"If you're a marine, how come you're not in uniform?' she asked, suspicious.

"As of a few months ago, I'm no longer active, but semper fi, and all that. Once a marine, always a marine," he said.

"If you like it so much, why aren't you still doing it?" she asked.

"That is a question that will require an extensive answer. It's more of a second date type thing," he said.

"This is not a first date," she informed him.

"We're having dinner, there's romance, soon there will be dancing. How is a first date any different?" he asked.

"Because usually the man asks and the woman is a willing participant," she said. "This is more like an elaborate kidnapping."

"This is way better than any kidnapping I've ever been a part of," he said. They took their seats, on opposite sides of Carolyn and David, to Jessamine's relief, and began eating. Jessamine split her time between chatting and laughing with Carolyn on her left and Carolyn's cousin on her right. After a while, Carolyn leaned over to speak to David and then leaned over to talk to Jessamine.

"Milo wants to know if you miss him."

"Don't feed the trolls," Jessamine admonished her.

"Oh, come on, Jess, he's cute, you're cute. Lighten up."

"Don't turn into one of those married women who tries to fix up all her single friends," Jessamine said.

"You're my only single friend now," Carolyn said.

"I could have lived forever without that information," Jessamine said, and they laughed. David nudged Carolyn who leaned close to him before coming back to Jessamine to relay her next message.

"Milo wants to know why you're nice to everyone but him," Carolyn said. "I'm becoming curious about that, too. I don't think I've ever seen you have such a visceral reaction to someone."

"He's so…smarmy."

"David likes him," Carolyn said, her tone somewhat defensive.

"Maybe David's been duped," Jessamine suggested.

"Nah, he's too smart for that," Carolyn said.

"Um, your adoring tone is making my skin crawl. Save it for the honeymoon, sister."

"All I'm saying is would it hurt you to give him a chance? I can't remember the last time you had a date. Can you?" Carolyn said.

"I'm busy," Jessamine said. "And I have high standards."

"You're a workaholic, and your standards are impossible. No one is ever going to measure up to your brothers, in your eyes."

"What a fun wedding. I can't wait until your first baby's christening so we can really delve into my flaws and debate my lingering childlessness," Jessamine said.

"You know I pick you apart because I love," Carolyn said.

"Try loving me a bit less," Jessamine said.

"I can't. You're so stinking lovable." Carolyn wrapped her arms around Jessamine's shoulders and squashed their cheeks together. David leaned over to whisper in Carolyn's ear, and she laughed. "Milo wants to know if he and I can trade places. I'm tempted to take him up on it."

"Do and you're dead to me."

"We've had a good run," Carolyn said.

"I'll take back my gift," Jessamine threatened. At Carolyn's request, she was going to decorate the master bedroom of their new house.

Carolyn let her go and turned to Milo. "No deal, sorry."

Eventually it was time to dance. Carolyn and David had their first dance and took turns dancing with their parents, and then it was time for the wedding party to join them on the floor. Everyone else paired off with alarming speed until it was only Milo and Jessamine left.

He held out his hand to her. "Come on, don't be shy. This will be a great story to tell our kids someday. You know a statistically large percentage of best men end up marrying maids of honor. That's fact."

Reluctantly she put her hand in his and allowed him to lead her onto the dance floor. It was a fast song that didn't require touching and she tried to pull her hand away. "Are you a germaphobe?" he asked.

"I don't know where your hands have been," she said.

"I could show you where they'd like to be," he offered.

"Either shut up and dance, or I'm out of here," she replied.

"Oh, you want to dance?" he asked.

"That's kind of the point of being on the dance floor," she said.

"But can you dance?" he asked and, for Jessamine, it was a painful reminder of her first ever dance, the one she'd shared with him.

"I can dance," she snapped, afraid he was going to attempt to repeat the lesson he'd given her sixteen years ago.

"Then let's dance," he said and took her hand and spun her so quickly she laughed out loud without thinking about it. He was a good dancer, and an even better lead, somehow making up for her inefficiencies as a mediocre dancer. Unlike a lot of people on the floor, they didn't simply stand near each other and gyrate to the music. He led her in a series of steps she suspected were some sort of variant on the mambo or the cha-cha with a bit of the hustle thrown in to keep it trendy. Jessamine hated to admit it, even to herself, but she was having a blast. And when the next two songs came on, they kept dancing until at last the DJ slipped in a slow song. Jessamine turned to go, but Milo used the hand he still held to hail her back again.

"Where are you going, MOH?" he asked. "Your best man still needs you."

"I will stay if you will act like a normal human being," she said.

"Define normal," he said.

"Keep your hands where my mother would approve them and stop trying to annoy me. It's like being pecked to death by a duck," she said.

"I'll try," he promised, and they started to dance. She liked that he held her in a formal dance pose with one hand on her waist and the other clasping her hand out to the side.

"Where did you learn to dance?" she asked.

"That's a first date question that requires a third date answer," he said.

"So mysterious," she said, smiling.

"Wait, are you flirting with me?" he asked.

"I've been known to do so when a man isn't trying to plow me under with unending chatter," she said.

"So you kind of meant it when you said you like the strong silent type?" he asked.

She nodded.

"Would you believe me if I told you my reaction to you has been something of an anomaly?" he asked.

She shook her head.

"Why not?" he asked.

"Because I don't trust you," she said.

"You're a challenge at every turn," he said and, as if to emphasize the point, used their joined hands to spin her before bringing her back again. "But you seem to like dancing."

"Who doesn't?" she asked.

"All the people sitting this one out," he said. Jessamine scanned the room and saw that, besides the bride and groom, there was only one other couple on the floor. Worse, most people were watching them and smiling, as if they were the ones in love.

"Oh," she said, embarrassed. "Well, this is awkward."

"Why?"

"I don't exactly like to be in the spotlight," she said.

"Aren't you on TV?" he asked.

"Because I enjoy my work, not because I want to be a star. Besides, I'm part of a team. I don't work solo."

"Did your brothers go on all the TV interviews with you?" he asked.

"No, they would hate that."

"Have they done the magazine interviews with you?" he asked.

"Some," she hedged.

"Newsflash: you're the star of the show."

"I'm not."

"Have you seen you? It's like you were made for television."

Her nose wrinkled. "Don't say things like that."

"Why not?" he asked.

"Because looks are so subjective, temporary, and shallow. Nothing should be based on appearances."

"You're probably right. Unfortunately beauty makes the world go 'round. Pretty people have it easier."

"I don't like that," she said.

"It's cute how you believe not liking something can make it not true," he said. "Have you ever dated an ugly man?"

"I've never dated a man *I* thought was ugly," she qualified.

"Ooh, you're deep," he said, then:

"'What are heavy? Sea-sand and sorrow,

What are brief? Today and tomorrow,

What are frail? Spring blossoms and youth,

What are deep? The ocean and truth,'" he quoted.

"So you're the kind of guy who spouts poetry," she said.

"Yes. Are you the kind of girl who is impressed by that?" he asked.

"Maybe," she said. "Who was it?"

"Christina Rossetti, underrated nineteenth century English poet," he said. "I read women, too, being that I'm not a chauvinist."

She was being lulled into lowering her guard with him. She knew it when he slid both his hands to her waist, inviting her to move her hands around his neck, and she complied.

"See, I'm not such a bad guy," he said, his thumbs smoothing gently along her waistline.

"Jury's still out," she said, although her glance fell to his lips for a brief second before meeting his eyes again.

"You're so unbelievably beautiful," he blurted. *Smooth, Milo,* he mentally chastised himself. *You're acting like a teenager with your first crush.*

The effect on Jessamine was immediate. He could practically see and feel her withdraw from him. One moment she was fully in his grasp, soft and yielding. The next she was a few inches away, cold and stiff.

"Excuse me, I have to do something," she said, and then she was gone.

Milo stood looking at the empty space she'd vacated. *What just happened here?* There was only one way to find out. Turning, he wound his way through the other couples now dancing and made his way outside. Jessamine stood on the sidewalk, phone in hand.

"What happened?" he asked.

"I needed to send an email," she replied, her back to him.

"At ten at night on a Saturday, in the middle of a wedding?" he said, incredulous.

"My job isn't really a respecter of time," she said, nonchalant, her back still to him. He pivoted around her and stepped into her line of sight.

"Jessamine, what was that?" he asked.

"What?" she said, eyes still on her phone. He was tempted to reach out and take it, but had a feeling that wouldn't go over well. Now that he could see her, he noticed she wasn't actually typing. She simply gripped the phone while she stared at it, trying hard to look at anything but him.

"One minute we were dancing, having a good time, and the next you ran away like all hellfire was chasing you," he said.

She looked up then, eyes sparking with anger. "I didn't run."

He started to reply when movement across the street caught his attention. "Hey, that guy is towing my car," he said.

"How is your car here when we rode in the limo?" Jessamine asked.

"Someone drove it from the church for me. Hey!" He ran across the street. After a moment's hesitation, Jessamine trotted after him. She was in good shape, but running in heels wasn't exactly her forte.

"What are you doing?" Milo demanded.

"Got a repo order for this vehicle," the man said, tossing his words out with careless abandon. It was clear he did the job often and had little regard for the vehicle's owner.

"Wait, no, I spoke to the lender. They were going to give me more time," Milo said.

The repo man shrugged and continued hooking up the car. "Got my orders. Unless you can pay right now, it's going on the truck."

"I didn't...I can't..." Milo stumbled.

"How much?" Jessamine interjected.

"A thousand bucks," the repo man replied in the same bored tone.

Jessamine searched through her tiny clutch purse and removed a credit card.

"Jessamine, no, that's not, I can't…" Milo continued to stumble for words.

"Which do you want more? Your pride or your car?" she asked.

Milo winced. "It's a thousand dollars. You barely know me."

"I know you well enough," she said, forcing her card toward the tow truck driver. He pulled out a card reader. "I want a receipt," she told him.

"Lady, this ain't Costco," he said. "Not like I got a printer in my truck."

"I'll settle for something hand written and dated," she told him. He opened his mouth to argue, took a look at her expression, and quickly cowered and wrote the receipt. Milo had to sign paperwork and wait for the man to unhook his car. By the time that was finished, Jessamine had disappeared. He made his way back to the wedding reception, almost reluctant to see her now, but he needn't have worried. She was nowhere in sight, disappeared as completely as if she had never been there at all.

CHAPTER 4

"How was Carolyn's wedding?" Jessamine's mother asked the next day at the weekly Samperi Sunday dinner.

"Sweet, sincere, romantic, beautiful. Everything a wedding should be," Jessamine said. Her cheek rested sleepily against her hand as she sat and watched her mother work in the kitchen.

"Must be wedding season—your brothers, all your friends..."

"Subtle, Ma. Why don't you get a couple of goats together and auction me to the highest bidder?" Jessamine said.

"Don't be ridiculous, dear. You know this is horse country," her mother replied.

"Why are we obsessing over Carolyn's wedding when we should be obsessing over mine?" Moss asked.

"And mine," Molly added, poking him.

"Shh, honey, the Samperis are talking," Moss replied, and she poked him again, this time where he was ticklish.

"Well, aren't you two adorable," Jessamine drawled.

"Bitter," Moss said, pretending to cough into his hand.

"Be nice to your sister. She's on wedding overload because everyone she has ever known is getting married. Except her," Mrs. Samperi said.

"I'm sorry, Jess," Moss said, putting his arm around her shoulders. "It isn't easy being literally the last single person on the planet."

She put him in a headlock. "Molly, you're in our prayers."

"I would say she's the lucky one, but we all know it's me," Moss said, pushing away from his sister to hug Molly.

Rolling her eyes, Jessamine left the kitchen. She entered the living room where she saw Lou sitting on Benny's lap in a recliner. They had just returned from a working honeymoon in Africa and were unnaturally tan. Vivian and Giovanni were sharing a game of chess, laughing and talking in their own intimate little bubble. Her father sat in his recliner cooing to Moss's baby, and Joe and Peaches sat on the couch a foot apart in stony silence. Jessamine plopped between them and linked arms with each.

"I love you guys," she declared.

They leaned in and rested their heads on hers. "How was Carolyn's wedding?" Peaches asked.

"Romantic," Jessamine said sourly.

Peaches chuckled. "Sorry. On a scale of one to throat punch everyone, where are you right now?"

"Ma's pressuring me to get married," Jessamine complained.

"Ma pressures about a lot of things," Joe said, his tone long-suffering.

"You have to find a happy place in your mind and go there," Peaches agreed.

"You must go there often," Jessamine observed. Peaches had been coming to their family dinners for twenty-three years, since Jessamine was only seven years old.

"I live there now," Peaches said. She was aiming for a light tone, but it came out heavy.

Jessamine wanted to let go of Joe and cling to Peaches. Her sister-in-law had been going through something for years that none of them understood, and nobody knew how to reach her, least of all Joe, whose helplessness was beginning to morph into resentment.

"I really do love y'all," Jessamine said instead, giving both their arms a squeeze.

"You're by far my favorite sister," Joe said, returning her squeeze.

"Mine too," Peaches said, making them laugh because she actually had a sister who wasn't a very nice person.

"Can we talk for a minute about the fact that Moss is getting married?" Jessamine said. The reality still hadn't sunk in for her. She was halfway between Moss and Joe, with five years both ways. If she was having a hard time accepting it, she couldn't imagine how Joe and Peaches must be feeling.

"You know he was two the first day I met him?" Peaches mused. "Oh, my lands, I don't think there has ever been a cuter baby, all those curls."

"He had to be cute because he was so rotten we would have killed him otherwise," Jessamine said.

"Truth," Joe said. "But really, though, I don't know how I'm going to get through the wedding, especially after almost losing Molly."

"I have got to find a date," Jessamine said. "There is no way I'm going through the mortification of showing up alone and having people ask me when it's my turn. I got enough of that at Benny's wedding to last a lifetime."

"People are completely lacking in tact," Peaches agreed. "I'm thinking of getting 'I'm Infertile' tattooed on my forehead so everyone will stop asking."

"Throat punches, all around," Jessamine said, holding up her fist for a bump.

"I'll throat punch, you slap them across the face," Peaches agreed, returning the bump.

"And I'll hold them all down so they can't get away," Joe said.

Jessamine's phone buzzed with a text. She pulled it out and read:

I miss you.

It was from an unassigned number she didn't recognize. She could have ignored it, but she felt doing so would be rude. Someone was missed; the least Jessamine could do was make sure the sentiment reached the correct person. So she texted a reply.

Sorry, wrong number.

The phone buzzed again with a reply. *No, Jessamine. I miss YOU.*

"That's weird," Jessamine said.

"Who was it?" Peaches asked.

"No one I recognize, but they said they miss me," Jessamine said. Someone knocked on the door. Everyone glanced at each other in surprise. Who could it be? All the Samperis and the Samperi extras were already present. People in the community knew Samperi Sunday was sacred. Who would arrive unannounced?

"Jessamine, get the door," her mother called.

Jessamine wanted to rebel at the command. She had four brothers. Why did she have to be the one to go? But, seeing as how she was an adult and now technically a guest in her mother's house, she peeled herself off the couch and answered the door.

Milo stood on the other side wearing a tie and holding a bouquet of flowers.

"Oh, it's you," Jessamine said. She stepped outside and closed the door hastily behind her.

"Not exactly the reception I was hoping for, but I'll take it," Milo said.

"Why are you here?" she asked.

"You left rather abruptly last night," he said.

"It had been a long day," she replied.

"Also there's the small fact that I now owe you a thousand dollars," he said.

"It's not a big deal," she said.

"It is to me," he replied.

"Maybe we can talk about it later," Jessamine suggested.

"When? Because I kind of have the feeling you're going to aggressively ignore me from now on."

"How does one aggressively ignore?" she asked.

"Something tells me you already know the answer to that question," he said.

"Did you just send me a text?" she asked, suspicious.

"How would I do that when I don't have your number?" he said.

Jessamine's palms were sweating. She had to get rid of him before...

"Well, who do we have here?" Her mother yanked open the door and poked her head out.

"I'm Milo Eliopoulos, Mrs. Samperi. These are for you," Milo said, bypassing Jessamine to thrust the flowers toward her mother.

"How very lovely, Milo. Please tell me you can stay for dinner," Mrs. Samperi said.

"Ma," Jessamine intoned.

"I'd love to," Milo said. "Your cooking is legendary, and I regret I've never had the pleasure."

"Aren't you sweet?" Mrs. Samperi replied, smiling. "Jess, show him the way." She turned and disappeared inside.

"I don't think you know what you're about to get into," Jessamine said.

"Pretty sure I do," Milo contradicted.

"My family is insane," Jessamine warned.

"I know that. Everyone knows that," he said. "I'm not afraid."

"That's what Daniel said before being tossed into the lion's den," she said.

"He mentioned your family by name? Weird," Milo said.

"Last chance to run away," Jessamine offered.

"Lead on," Milo said. He followed her inside and closed the door.

CHAPTER 5

*M*ilo was lying, at least a little bit. The Samperis did intimidate him. They had always been above him, in terms of class. While his family had been stuffed into a tiny bungalow on the wrong side of town, the Samperis' sprawling mansion sat on acres of land. There was a bedroom for each child, along with a huge barn where the family used to live. In short, they were loaded. The only thing that made them approachable, at least to Milo, was the fact that their father, Pete Samperi, had started the business from the ground up with only skill and determination. They worked hard, and they worked with their hands. Milo hadn't respected that when he was a kid, but he did now.

He tagged behind Jessamine as she led him into the grand entry, past the kitchen, and into a dining room that was approximately the size of his entire house. All the family was there and seated. Everyone turned collectively to stare at him, and it took all of his military training not to turn tail and run.

Joe and Peaches, Benny and Lou he knew from school. Jessamine's younger brothers he recognized through family resemblance, but they had been too young for him to remember. One of the younger siblings wore tortoiseshell glasses and inspected him as if he were a lab report.

Beside him sat a petite brunette with long, lustrous hair. The other brother had a shaggy mop of curls and smiled at Milo in what could best be described as pure orneriness. Beside him sat another long-haired brunette with big, brown eyes and a slightly upturned nose. Jessamine seemed to be the only unattached one in the family. *Interesting.*

"Milo Eliopoulos, how very, very interesting," Lou said.

"Hello, Lou," he replied. She had been a year behind him school, but they'd shared two classes and a study hall together. While not technically friends, he had always been amused by her brash, outspoken approach to life.

"Hey, Milo," Peaches added, her voice as soft and sweet as he remembered. Joe and Peaches had been two years ahead of him. He had always liked them as well as Benny, but now the two men were looking at him with matching frowns of disapproval. He wanted to tell them he wasn't the same stupid kid he had been, but how was he supposed to say that with everyone gawking at him as they were? Jessamine certainly did nothing to ease his discomfort. If anything, she looked even more uncomfortable than he was. She sat. He slid into the empty space beside her. The elder Mr. Samperi said a blessing, and food began to pass.

"Quick question: who is Milo?" the curly haired Samperi brother asked.

"He went to school with us," Benny supplied, ever the diplomat. "How have you been, Milo?"

"I'm hanging in there," Milo replied. "I thought you were in some other country."

"I was, but I got malaria and had to come home," Benny supplied.

"I'm Moss," the curly brother supplied. "This is my fiancée, Molly."

"Milo Eliopoulos," Milo said, nodding and smiling. His eyes fell questioningly on the brother with glasses.

"Giovanni," he said. "And my wife, Vivian."

"Nice to meet you," Milo said.

"What are you doing here?" Moss asked.

"Mossimo," Mrs. Samperi snapped.

"I didn't mean it in a rude way. I was asking out of curiosity. Are we working for you now? Renovating something, building something? Is Jess designing a space for you?"

"No. Jessamine and I met up this weekend at Carolyn's wedding, and I stopped by to talk with her about something," Milo said. Moss continued to stare at him in open speculation while the other three brothers relaxed slightly, secure in the knowledge he wasn't about to abscond with their sister for any nefarious purpose.

"I find it so curious how my children keep finding people who have lived around here forever, and yet we never knew them," Mrs. Samperi noted. "Were you and Jessamine friends in school?"

"I was sandwiched between Joe and Benny. Jessamine and I never had the pleasure to encounter each other in school," Milo said. To his left, Jessamine choked and began coughing furiously into a napkin.

"Scampi in my throat," she gasped. "No one panic." She picked up her water and gulped a few sips.

"No one will," Moss assured her.

"Did you have a date for the wedding?" Mrs. Samperi asked Milo, and Jessamine coughed harder.

"Easy, Ma. Jess is going to crack a rib," Moss added.

"No," Milo said. "But a date wouldn't have been the easiest thing, what with being the best man, and all."

"You mean you were the best man while Jess was maid of honor?" Mrs. Samperi said. "You got to walk down the aisle together?"

"And dance," Milo added helpfully.

"Statistically speaking, a lot of best men end up marrying maids of honor," Lou said.

"Really?" Mrs. Samperi asked, leaning forward with interest.

"Thanks, Lou, that's helpful information," Jessamine said.

"I think I read that, too," Vivian chimed in.

"Did anyone watch the game last night? I missed it, for obvious reasons," Jessamine said.

"Because you were dancing with Milo?" Moss guessed.

"Don't," Mrs. Samperi admonished, banging her spoon on the table when Jessamine picked up a piece of shrimp to chuck at Moss's head.

"That shrimp is seventeen dollars a pound. Throw the noodles, I can practically make them for free."

"So, Milo," Mr. Samperi boomed from the opposite end of the table. This was it, the moment when they would ask him what he did for a living. "Who did you like in last night's game, the Wildcats or the Cardinals? And, no pressure, but you're going to lose about half the table, no matter how you answer."

"Believe it or not, Mr. Samperi, I don't actually follow sports that closely," Milo said. "Sorry."

"Why are you sorry? All those men running around butting heads. Ridiculous," Mrs. Samperi said.

"We were discussing basketball, Marie," Mr. Samperi said.

"All those men running around in little shorts, doodling a ball," Mrs. Samperi amended, shaking her head.

"It's just for fun, Ma, a distraction," Jessamine said.

"A distraction from what? What would you need distracted from?" Mrs. Samperi demanded.

"It's a mystery, Ma," Giovanni said, his tone dry.

"I don't like that, SpongeBob Secret Pants," Mrs. Samperi replied, pointing a wooden spoon at him.

For his part, Milo was trying hard not to laugh. The Samperis were funnier than he imagined they'd be. For some reason he had thought of them as being all work and no play types, the same as Jessamine. Though, to be fair, he hardly knew her. Just because that was his first impression of her didn't mean it was true.

"Giovanni and Vivian eloped and kept it a secret from the family," Jessamine leaned closer to whisper to Milo. "Ma still hasn't forgiven them."

He nodded, trying to keep his expression neutral. She smelled amazing; she looked amazing; she *was* amazing. He hadn't been this crazily attracted to a woman since…had he ever been this attracted to a woman? A cry erupted from the other room, startling him.

Moss poked Molly. "Your baby's awake."

"The one I got up twice in the night with?" Molly asked, poking him in return.

"That's the one," he said, poking her again.

"For pity's sake, I'll get her," Jessamine declared, rising.

"Don't, stop, come back," Moss said softly, making no move to leave the table. Jessamine returned a minute later carrying a baby who, despite her earlier cries, was now smiling congenially at the room at large. Two tiny teeth poked through her bottom gums.

"This is Bella," Jessamine introduced Milo. "She's our sweetheart." As soon as Jessamine sat, the baby lunged for Milo who reached for her instinctively. "You don't have to."

"I love babies," he assured her. "I'm an old hat." She studied him, probably wondering why he was so comfortable with babies, but he paid her no mind as he cuddled and cooed to the baby, already an extrovert who knew how to flirt, if her glowing smiles and giggles of delight were any indication. He became so wrapped up in the baby's infectious laugh that he tuned out everyone else until suddenly realizing that everyone was now watching him in silence.

"Well, looks like we've found a new backup babysitter," Moss declared, ending the silence. Milo turned the baby around to face the table. For a few seconds she entertained herself grabbing for his silverware, then she caught sight of Molly and lunged for her instead. Milo stood to hand her the baby, accidentally knocking into Jessamine in the process.

"Sorry," he apologized as he sat. He patted her knee, resisting the urge to let his hand linger. Instinctively he knew she wouldn't like it, and especially not in full view of her family. He didn't know her well enough to understand her reactions, nor how to break beyond her icy exterior. *Yet*, he amended. He didn't know her well enough *yet*.

After that, conversation turned to Moss's upcoming wedding. Since Benny was the one to start talking, Milo assumed he was giving Jessamine an out by turning attention away from her and Milo. When the meal was finished, Milo helped carry plates and bowls to the kitchen. Somehow during that time, he lost Jessamine again. Thinking she was in the bathroom, he waited in the giant kitchen for her to return. When she didn't show, he eventually determined that she was once again avoiding him.

"She's in the tree house," Mrs. Samperi supplied, nodding her head toward the back window. "You'll have to go to her, if you want to see her." She paused and seemed to be fishing for her words. "It sounds bad for a mother to say this to a man about her daughter, but after I say it, I think you'll understand what I mean. With Jessamine, you can't take no for an answer."

Milo smiled. "I sensed that about her. Thank you, Mrs. Samperi." He let himself out the back door and scanned the horizon for a tree house, hoping it was anywhere but up a tree. Approximately a football field away, he spotted it atop a giant oak. Of course it literally had to be up a tree, and not just up a tree but at the top of a huge tree, easily two stories high. Sighing, he made his way across the yard.

 ilo sighed again when he reached the base of the tree house. At least it was stairs and not a ladder, though it was a daunting amount of stairs and they were steep. *Don't look down,* he admonished himself. Grasping the handrail as if it were a lifeline, he made his way up top.

The ladder ended at a trapdoor. Would it be unlocked? Milo pushed on it, his heart flopping almost nervously when it opened. He poked his head through and saw Jessamine sitting on the floor, her back to him as she stared at the wall. He let himself in, taking care not to let the door slam in his wake, and sat down next to her.

"Are we waiting for the wall to do something magic?" he asked.

"No."

"You disappeared," he accused.

"Sorry, I needed an out for a minute and I guess I lost track of time. This is a good place to think," she replied.

"It is that," he agreed, looking around the space. For a tree house, it was large and spacious. He should have expected nothing less from a family of builders, but he was still surprised.

"This was the first thing I built when I was a kid," she told him.

"You built this?" he exclaimed.

"Yes, my dad let me nail these three boards." She leaned forward on her knees and touched the wall in front of them. "It was my first taste of the business, and I fell in love. From then on, I couldn't wait to get my hands on a hammer again. My brothers let me decorate. My mom helped me sew these curtains." He should have known she had done the decorating. Even though it was almost puritanically sparse, what was present matched and flowed as if a designer had done it, a tiny eight-year-old designer in training.

"About the money," he began unable to stand it any longer. "I'm not the type of person who doesn't pay his bills."

"I never said you were," she replied.

"You must have been thinking it," he said.

"Must I?" she asked, turning to him with a coy smile he could in no way interpret.

"You saw my car being repossessed. It was the logical conclusion. The thing is that I had to leave the marines rather hastily, due to unforeseen circumstances. I didn't have another job lined up. I've been working on finding one, and I have some prospects. In the meantime, things are a bit skint."

"Skint?" she questioned.

"A British expression meaning broke," he informed her. "Skint. Here, I'll use it in a sentence. I'm so skint I had to let the most interesting woman I've met in a decade pay for my car, and now I have to figure out a way to pay her back."

She smiled at him and lightly bumped his shoulder. "Believe it or not, money's not a huge concern for me at this point in my life."

"Really? It's almost like you're a huge reality TV star or something," he said. After arriving home last night, he had Googled her, which had only increased his fascination with her. She was legitimately famous, an internet and television sensation.

"Please, tell me more about how fabulous I am. It's my favorite," she said.

"Oh, I plan to. In the meantime, let's talk about a timeline for my repayment," he said.

She rolled her eyes. "I don't need a timeline. You'll get there when you get there."

"Is there a reason you're being so understanding and patient with me, Miss Samperi?" he asked, leaning forward slightly.

She leaned forward, too, her face a hairsbreadth from his. "Yes."

"Are you going to tell me what it is?" he asked. His hand itched to reach up, to brush the hair off her cheek.

"You're a vet," she said, sitting back out of his reach.

He blinked. "That's it? Because I'm a vet?"

"What other reason do you need? I have nothing but respect for the military, and I know coming back is a hard transition." She held up her fist for him to bump. "Props."

"Props and a fist bump? Are we buds now? Bros?"

"You're cranky today. I might have liked you better last night," she said, a barely repressed smile the only hint of her teasing.

"You're kind of driving me crazy here, Samperi," he said and this time he did reach up to push the wild strands away from her face. Her hair was like everything else about her—unpredictable and uncontained with a mind of its own.

"Milo," she said his name on a breathless whisper, sounding uncertain. He hesitated, not sure how far he should push her. If only he knew her better, if only he understood what made her tick, then he would know when and how far to push her. They sat frozen a few seconds, staring, their faces mere inches apart. Tentatively, she reached a hand toward his face, and then suddenly he knocked her to the ground, the back of her head cradled protectively in his hand to absorb the shock of landing.

"Um, what the what?" she asked, her voice a mixture of shock and irritation.

"Gunshot," Milo replied. His heart was hammering, his chest heaving while blood thundered in his ears.

"Milo, it's deer gun season in Kentucky. It would be weird if people weren't shooting," she said. When he remained frozen atop her, she did put up a hand, her fingers gently scraping along his scalp as she sifted his hair. "Are you okay?"

"I…" Milo stuttered. As the panic ebbed, embarrassment began. "I'm kind of used to responding to that sound a certain way."

"It's okay," Jessamine said, her voice as soft and soothing as he'd ever heard it. "We're all right. Everyone is safe. It's fine." All the while her hand smoothed gently over his head, calming him. Her other hand joined in. She was petting him as if he were a nervous collie, but he found he lacked the ability to care. Jessamine Samperi was in his arms, her hands in his hair, and—at least for the moment—she made no attempt to get away.

"Do you have PTSD?" she asked after a moment of silence. "Is that too personal? Life with my mother has done terrible things to my internal filter."

"It's fine. To answer your question, I'm not sure. You get so used to acting a certain way in combat that it becomes ingrained, a sort of muscle memory. Gunshot equals everybody hit the floor."

"Thanks for protecting me. Too bad the local deer can't say the same." She winked at him, one of her multi-colored, impossibly-lashed sparkling eyes, and his brain turned to mush.

Want, want, want, need, need, need, was the only thing he could seem to think or feel at the moment. It didn't help that they were still pressed together, her arms around his neck, her hands in his hair.

"Go out with me tonight," he blurted.

She tensed. "Like, a date? On a Sunday?"

"Dancing," he said, his voice a little croaky. "There's a club in Lexington that does swing dancing on Sundays."

"Swing dancing?" she echoed. Was that a hint of excitement he detected?

He nodded, smiling. "Swing dancing."

"Do you know how to swing dance?" she asked.

He nodded again, slower this time.

"Yowza," she said, staring up at him with big eyes.

"Yowza?" he repeated, his smile widening. "What does that mean?"

"I'm not explaining my yowza to you," she said. "Also, you're still on top of me."

"Was that an observation or a complaint?" he said.

"It's a request for oxygen," she said.

"It would seem we're at an impasse," he said.

"How so?" she asked.

"You want oxygen which, by the way, needy much? I had no idea you were such a high-maintenance diva. And I want…well, I think we both know what I want," he said.

"A kick in the teeth? Because I have one with your name on it, the very second you release me," she said. The hint of a smile was still there, on her face and in her words. He was beginning to realize she was far less serious than he gave her credit for. Now that he understood and had met her family, he wondered how much of what she said was actually true or mere bluster.

"Hmm, now I have even less incentive to release you," he said. "We fit remarkably well, don't you think? It's almost like we were made for each other."

"No, it's more like my spine is molding and conforming to the wood slats beneath me, thereby making room for you to squish me," she said.

"You said 'thereby.' No one talks like that in the middle of a highly charged romantic encounter."

"Speaking of highly charged, have you seen my Taser? I seemed to have misplaced it, and I find I need it desperately just now," she said.

"Your Taser says no, but your eyes say yes," he said.

"Why do I have a feeling you've said that to a lot of women?" she asked.

"You'd be shocked if you knew how few, Taser pun intended."

"I wouldn't be shocked. I'd be downright amazed and flabbergasted. A guy who looks like you, who acts like you, is suddenly claiming to be a no-hitter with the ladies?"

"How do I look?" he asked, feigning innocence.

"Currently? Like the guy who's going to be charged with homicide after I'm found suffocated to death beneath you," she said, squirming uncomfortably.

"You really want me to get off you, to let you go?" he asked, his eyes boring into hers.

Before she could answer, the trap door popped open and Moss poked his head through. "Well, this is awkward," he said.

"It's a long story," Jessamine said.

"Pretty sure I've read that book before. Mine ended with a baby," he said.

"What do you want?" Jessamine snapped.

"Ma wants to know if Milo wants an *affogato*," Moss said.

"Tell Ma yes," Jessamine said and, mercifully, Moss disappeared the way he came.

"What's an *affogato*?" Milo asked. He rolled to the side and sat up, lending Jessamine a hand to do the same.

"It's a scoop of gelato in an espresso, but it doesn't matter. When my mother offers you food, you always say yes or get on her bad side forever," Jessamine said.

"Is there a particular reason you don't want me on your mother's bad side forever?" he asked, still grasping her hand.

She plucked it free. "Because she's scarier than a rabid badger when she's upset."

With effort, he refrained from saying how much that sounded like her. "About the other thing, I will pay you back. It may take longer than I would like, but I will do it."

"I know you will," she said. She gave his hand a squeeze. He wanted to bring it to his lips, to kiss her palm. Instead he settled for a more impersonal kiss on the back of her hand before letting go. His heart kept telling him to go for it while his brain kept holding him back. So far, that was the part of him he was choosing to follow.

Jessamine picked up his tie, letting the silky length of it glide through her fingers. Milo barely dared to breathe. "Why a tie?" she asked.

"I thought your mom would like it," he said.

"I like it," she admitted. "A man who dresses well is kind of sexy."

"Are you allowed to say 'sexy' on a Sunday?" he asked.

"Depends on the context," she said, her eyes still on the tie. "So, dancing."

"Dancing. Are you in?"

"As long as it's only dancing and I can take my car and meet you there, yes," she said.

"Absolutely," he agreed. They left the tree house. Milo made sure she was in front of him. Ladies first was the gentlemanly thing to do, but his insistence had nothing to do with manners and everything to do with hiding how tightly he gripped the handrail on the way down.

They made polite goodbyes to her family, and then they were on their way to the dance club—in separate cars like strangers. Was she embarrassed to be seen in his ratty clunker (the one she now technically owned)? He didn't think that was it. He was beginning to realize that Jessamine was kinder, funnier, and softer than he'd first believed. One thing hadn't changed since his first impression, though: whatever the situation, Jessamine Samperi wanted more than anything to be the one in complete control.

CHAPTER 7

What am I doing here? That was the question Jessamine had been asking herself the last two hours. Yesterday Milo had been an annoyance to be avoided. Today he was her dance partner. *How?*

Was it because he was such an amazing dancer? Maybe. Jessamine had a weakness for dancing and for men who did it well. He still hadn't explained how or where he learned to dance. Was it part of Marine training? Doubtful.

Friday when she heard his voice in the bar, she had known immediately who he was. It had felt like the last sixteen years were stripped away and she was once again the uncertain fourteen year old, the one with the too-big nose. She had wanted to punch him for the pain he inflicted on that little girl. Then, as the weekend continued, she wanted to punch him for different reasons, not least of which was the incessant way he pecked at her. And then somehow everything began to shift, to slide out of her tightfisted grasp. That was the part she still wasn't clear on? What exactly happened?

Milo was as attractive as ever. In high school, he had smoldered with a bad boy intensity. The smolder had given away to plain old handsomeness, well on its way to becoming distinguished, thanks to a smidgeon of salt among the pepper of his hair. But in Jessamine's world of four handsome brothers, good looks were nothing special. It wasn't physical attraction that drew her to him. So what was it?

As a kid, she had been drawn to his naughtiness, almost titillated by it. Now she knew better. Bad boys often grew up to be bad men, and no one had time or energy for that, least of all her. Milo didn't seem bad anymore, though. Now he radiated an almost Zen-like calmness, one that couldn't be had unless it was earned. What had happened to smooth off his rough edges? Time? Combat? Or something else, something hidden?

The same air of mystery surrounded him as it had in high school, only this time without the danger. Jessamine knew next to nothing about him. Despite attending the same small school in the same small town, they hadn't traveled in the same circles. Until he told her he'd become a marine, Jessamine had had no idea what happened to him after he graduated. She could ply Carolyn for information, but she was on her honeymoon. And Jessamine didn't want her oldest friend to get the wrong idea. She wasn't interested in Milo; she was merely curious.

"Ready for a break?" Milo leaned forward and spoke in her ear. They had been dancing for nearly the last two hours without pause—fast, lively, blessedly impersonal swing dancing. He had held her hand and occasionally touched her waist to push her away or pull her back in again after a spin. Otherwise there had been no touching or conversation and Jessamine couldn't remember the last time she'd had so much fun.

"You are in amazingly good shape," Milo noted as they grabbed a couple of drinks and slid into a booth.

"Sixteen years of construction work does a body good," she remarked.

"You have no idea how much I want to leer at you and say, 'I'll say it does,'" Milo said.

"Thanks for refraining," Jessamine said.

"I thought you were the designer now, sort of hands off."

"I still like to do what I can, when I have the time. My dad firmly believes that working with our hands is better than any therapy. It's hard to shake that training. So when I don't have time to do stuff for clients, I do stuff for myself, for fun."

"Like what?"

"I used to flip houses. Now I renovate my own space, as many times as it takes to get it right," she said.

"You flipped houses? On your own?"

"Mostly. I flipped my first when I was eighteen, a tiny little rundown cottage. Occasionally I have to contract some things out. My brother Joe is better at pouring concrete than I am. I can do it, mind, but he does it better."

She said the last part as a challenge, as if Milo were questioning her competence because she wasn't as good as her brother at something. She took a sip of tea and sat back as if waiting for him to have a certain reaction. He wondered how other men had reacted to her in the past. Was her competence a challenge to their masculinity? Milo supposed he could understand, but he found her so fascinating, so incredibly alluring, there was no room for insecurity.

"If concrete's not your specialty, what is?" he asked. "What do you do better than your brothers, besides design?"

"Carpentry," she admitted, almost shyly now.

"What have you made?" he asked.

"A lot of things, but I enjoy cabinetry the most. There's something particularly soothing about the combination of form and function. Seeing random boards suddenly turn into an assembled cabinet like magic is incredibly gratifying. Smoothing rough edges, joining corners, cutting, sanding, staining. It's the best."

"*Wow*," he mouthed.

"What?" she asked, tensing again.

"You make carpentry sound sexy, and I didn't know that was possible. If you'd been my high school shop teacher instead of Mr. Oblecker, I might have made a birdhouse that didn't collapse, and that house sparrow might be alive today."

She laughed. "Poor Mr. Oblecker. That man hated teaching and hated children."

"Did you take shop?"

"No, I lived it. Joe took it. It didn't go well."

"Why not?" Milo asked.

"Because Mr. Oblecker was lazy and cut corners in a way my father would never allow. Joe naively called him on it and became public enemy number one. After that my dad was so disgusted he never let any of the rest of us take the class."

"That sounds like him. I wonder if he's still teaching," Milo mused.

"Only if they made him a zombie. He died about ten years ago," Jessamine said.

"Oh. I sort of lost track of everything after graduation," he said.

"You've been a little busy, what with defending the free world and all," she said.

"If I didn't know better, I would think you might be flirting with me right now," he said.

"Good thing you know better," she said. She downed the last of her sweet tea and indicated the dance floor with a nod. "Are you ready to get back out there?"

"Where does your energy come from? And if you say you're a witch, know it's not automatically a deal breaker," he said.

"I have a gusto for life," she said. "And dancing." She slid out of the booth, took his hand, and led him back to the floor. Swing dancing had given way to the Charleston. Milo wasn't good at it, the first dance he hadn't been able to do seamlessly. Jessamine couldn't stop the bubbles of laughter that erupted every time he had to try to splay his knees and move them back and forth. Eventually she gave up and doubled over with the giggles.

"You're blatantly making fun of me in a room full of people," he complained.

"I'm sorry," she said, wiping her streaming eyes. "Sort of. But it's so refreshing to see you struggle. You're such a good dancer otherwise."

"Flattery will get you everywhere," he said. The song switched to a regular slow dance. Without permission, he pulled her closer and started to dance.

"This has been fun, Milo. Thank you," Jessamine said.

"Please believe me when I say the pleasure was all mine, except the Charleston. Let's never speak of that again."

She giggled and he smiled. Before tonight, he definitely wouldn't have pegged her for a giggler. "Maybe we could do this again sometime, make it a kind of regular thing," he suggested.

"Dancing?" she clarified.

"Sure," he said. "To begin with."

One time Milo caught a mole in his back yard. Jessamine was now wearing the same expression as that mole.

"Um..." she began. He was intensely curious to hear what she might say, but they were interrupted before she could find more words. Someone stumbled up beside him and laid a hand on his shoulder.

"Milo, man, I haven't seen you in forever."

"Found the bar did you, Stu?" Milo asked. The guy reeked of scotch or maybe it was rum. Maybe both.

Stu laughed. "Yeah." He looked at Jessamine, confused. "Hey, that's not your wife."

"Uh," now it was Milo's turn to stutter. He looked like someone who had been caught in a very big lie. Jessamine picked up his hand and looked at his ring finger. It had the tan line of someone who had recently removed a wedding ring. How had she not noticed that before? Because she hadn't been looking or because she hadn't wanted to realize? She turned and walked away.

"Jessamine, wait," he called, but she didn't. He had been caught; he was as much of an untrustworthy creep as she had first believed. She knew there was something about him she couldn't put her finger on. How had she fallen for his shtick? *Married.* Of all the gross possibilities, this was by far the grossest. Where was his wife now? Was she home, wondering where her husband was? Jessamine huffed in frustration. She couldn't wait to get home and wash the stench of him off her.

"Wait, please," Milo called, jogging to keep up with her as she grabbed her coat and stormed to the exit.

She didn't reply, and she certainly didn't stop. Right now she had the energy and determination of a freight train, and nobody better get in her way.

"Jessamine," Milo said softly. He rested his hand on her shoulder, and she tensed. "Can I please explain to you what happened?"

She whirled to face him. "How does it require an explanation? You're either married or you're not. There's no in between, no gray area."

"There is, actually," he said.

"Not in my world. I don't involve myself with married men," she said and turned her back on him, effectively ending the conversation.

Being Milo, he didn't see it that way and took a few steps closer until he was right behind her. "If you would let me explain, I think you would understand," he said.

She spun to face him again, furious. "You don't know me well enough to realize that you need to back off and leave me be *right now*."

"I can't do that until you let me explain."

She took a step back and bumped the brick wall of the dance hall. "Go away."

He took a step closer until they were once again inches apart. "No. Hear me out, please."

"Go away," she reiterated, her tone icier and more direct.

And then Milo made the fatal mistake of leaning in to kiss her. And Jessamine slapped him across the face, hard. "Did you misunderstand me?" she hissed. "This isn't 1954. When a woman says back off, it's not an invitation to kiss her."

He put his palm to his cheek, staring at her in shock. "You hit me."

"You had it coming," she said. "And, so we're clear, I never want to see or hear from you again." With that, she stormed to her car and drove away, leaving Milo staring after her, his hand still pressed to his cheek in surprise.

CHAPTER 8

On Monday, Jessamine was ready for work, sweet, blessed, mind-encompassing work. Filming began again, and it took all of her focus and then some. It didn't always go in a linear fashion. They filmed a blitz of footage and then it was up to the production crew to edit the raw film into a workable storyline. They were extremely good at it. When the cameras first showed up, Jessamine was convinced the show would be a flop. Who would want to watch endless scenes of them working? Then, when they had their first screening, she began to realize what a talented crew could do. Somehow they had put everything together so it played like a story. Furthermore, they had captured each of their personalities; Joe's steady calmness, her tendency to take charge and boss her brothers, Benny's placid good nature, Giovanni's perfectionistic precision, and Moss's lovable orneriness. The only embarrassing part of the process was how many screaming arguments they had. She feared the viewing public would believe they were at war, but somehow the reality came through—the fact that they had been communicating that way for so long that they had no idea they were doing it. No one had been angry during any of the screaming rows, a fact that was somehow able to come through via the magic of selective editing. In fact, the most pervasive elements of the show were fun and family togetherness, and Jess had been immensely relieved that the truth of their relationships had been revealed. She had even started to see unlicensed t-shirts pop up on the internet with a picture of a hearing aid and the words "Screaming Samperis."

"Tell them we're not always that loud," her mother had insisted the first time she saw the show.

"It's okay, Ma, they can probably hear you themselves from here," Giovanni had said, pressing his hand to his ear as he sat beside his mother.

"People don't really think we yell all the time, do they?" Mrs. Samperi had asked. She surveyed Vivian, Lou, Peaches and Molly. "What do you girls think? You're objective. Are we loud?"

"Not compared to jet turbines, foghorns, and lawnmowers," Lou had dared to say, earning snickers from the remaining in-laws.

Mrs. Samperi frowned. "I don't get it. We don't seem loud to me."

"We're fine," Mr. Samperi boomed. He was the loudest and most clueless of the group.

Now, as filming for the next few episodes resumed, Jessamine was once again cognizant of the yelling. Currently Moss and Giovanni were arguing over who had left a container of mastic open, allowing it to dry out.

"I have never left a container open in my life. I check the lids religiously," Giovanni said.

"Clearly you owe the mastic gods a sacrifice because you let them down big time," Moss replied.

"Of the two of us, who is more likely to leave a container open?" Giovanni demanded.

"Which of us was tiling on Friday?" Moss asked.

"You were," Giovanni said.

"How do you know that unless it was you who framed me?" Moss asked.

Giovanni used his thumb to rub the spot in the middle of his forehead that only Moss seemed able to activate. "Go to the truck and get more mastic before I bludgeon you."

"I'll cover for you this time, but try to be more responsible," Moss said before disappearing to the truck.

Giovanni made eye contact with Jessamine and shook his head. *"I swear,"* he mouthed.

Laughing, Jessamine returned to her sketch of the kitchen. How married was she to the cabinet placement? Moving them would require adding a support beam. Joe wouldn't be happy, but she could gain a few more cabinets if she did so. She closed her eyes, trying to picture it the revised way. As if Joe could read her mind, he called her name, sounding distressed.

"Jess? Where are you?" he called.

"The kitchen," she yelled. "Such as it is." For now, it was a mass of studs and bare wiring. It wouldn't begin to resemble a kitchen for a few more days.

Joe arrived in the kitchen looking flushed and flustered. Jessamine was immediately on the alert. "What's the matter?" she asked.

"You need to come with me," he said.

Her heart dropped. "What is it? What's wrong? Did something happen to Mom and Dad?"

The cameras seemed to zoom in on her, and she wanted to shoo them away. Her biggest complaint about being constantly on film was that they seemed always to be looking for some hint of action or drama. If she was about to learn of some dire family tragedy, she didn't want it on record for all of humanity to gaze at her emotion.

"No, of course not. Nothing like that. Everything is fine, but I need you to come with me. Right now."

"Joe, what…"

"Just come," he said, taking her arm and practically frog marching her to his truck. He opened the door, tossed her inside, scanned the horizon, and then got behind the wheel and took off.

"Can you tell me what's going on now?" she asked. Of all of them, Joe enjoyed the cameras the least. Had he been waiting until they were out of range to fill her in on the details?

"I got a call from Molly," he said.

"Okay," she prompted.

"She opened a letter today for you that was…weird."

"Oh," Jessamine said, laughing in relief. Since the show aired, they had fielded the occasionally strange fan mail. "Was it like when that old lady mailed Moss a lock of her gray hair with a creepy proposal?"

"No, this was something different. I've never heard Molly this freaked out before," he said.

"She's getting married in a few weeks. Maybe it's stress," Jessamine suggested.

"Have you ever known Molly to freak out before?" he asked her. "She calmly returned to work four days after being almost stabbed to death."

"Good point," Jessamine said. "Still, how bad could it be?"

"We're meeting her at the police station," he said.

"Are you joking?" she asked.

He shook his head. "Jess, she sounded petrified. I could barely understand her she was crying so hard. She opened the letter, grabbed up Bella, and drove to the police station."

"Yeesh," Jessamine said, her chest filling with a mixture of dread and anxiety. What could scare steady Molly so badly?

After what seemed like forever, they arrived at the police station. After initially getting the runaround, they were soon ushered to an interview room. Molly sat inside, clutching Bella and talking softly. She had calmed considerably, and Jessamine began to think perhaps it had all been a big misunderstanding.

"What's up?" Jessamine asked, going forward to sit beside Molly. Joe sat on her other side and clasped his hands on the table, leaning forward in earnest anticipation.

"There was a letter addressed to you, typed with no return address. Right away I figured it must be something bad because that's pretty suspicious. So I was braced for some kind of weirdness, but this, Jess…" she trailed off helplessly and gave Bella another hug.

"Molly, what is it?" Jessamine asked.

"It was…" Molly started, but the door was opened and a detective walked in.

"Miss Samperi, thank you for coming in today. I'm Detective

George Harris. I asked your secretary to summon you because I feel that this matter is incredibly urgent."

"Can you please explain to me what is going on?" Jessamine asked.

"Molly opened the letter today and saw these." He tossed a handful of photos onto the table in front of her. Jessamine saw herself staring up at her.

"Someone's been taking pictures of me," she said, still not terribly alarmed. People had surreptitiously been snapping her photo since the show began, a weird side effect of becoming famous.

"Keep going," the detective said.

Jessamine shuffled through the stack, looking at herself in various outfits and in various unaware poses. She stopped short and froze when she reached the last one. In it, she was asleep in her bed, and the photo had been taken from less than a foot away.

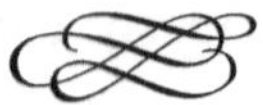

CHAPTER 9

The phone woke Milo. He checked the time and couldn't believe how late he'd slept. His former drill sergeant would have turned him inside out for being such a slacker. He needed to find a job, pronto.

"Hello," he said, trying hard not to sound like he had just woken up.

"Milo, this is Detective George Harris. I have a bit of a situation here, and someone gave me your name as a possible solution."

He frowned, wondering in what universe he would be the answer to anyone's problem. "I heard you're recently out of the armed forces and in need of a job. I may have a temporary assignment for you, if you're interested."

Milo perked up. "I'm interested. What's up?"

"I need to hire private security for someone. A woman has been receiving threats. We're in collusion with the FBI and hoping to have things wrapped up soon, but in the meantime she needs looking after."

"Is it a domestic violence type thing?" Milo asked reluctantly. He had zero desire to insert himself into something so volatile.

"Nothing like that," the detective assured him. "A local who has recently become famous has picked up a stalker, and the threat is fairly credible. Her family is friends with the chief, and you know how that goes. We like to take care of our own."

Milo gripped the phone. "What's her name?"

"Jessamine Samperi. I take it you're familiar with the Samperis. Are you okay?"

"Fine," Milo choked when he could reasonably stop coughing. "Throat tickle. I'm familiar." He paused and cleared his throat again, gulping a sip of water. "Does she know you're calling me?"

"We told her we're going to get security. She's not happy about it. We didn't tell her who."

"Good," Milo said. "I'm interested in meeting with her. Do me a favor and don't tell her it's me, okay?"

"Will do," the detective said. "We're anxious to get this wrapped up. Being that she's famous now kind of puts our whole department in the spotlight. We can't afford for this to go wrong, you know what I'm saying?"

"I hear you loud and clear," Milo said. They set up the meeting time and Milo hung up the phone, smiling as he stared into space. *Well, well, well.* And he thought his life after the marines would be boring.

⚷

The days following the letter were an exhausting blur, not only for Jessamine, but for all of the Samperis. Everyone was on high alert in case anyone else received another letter. No one did, and Jessamine received nothing else. She changed out the locks on her door, had a new security system installed and, at their insistence, slept at her parents' house while the investigation was ongoing.

Being home again after so long living on her own was strange, unnerving, and frustrating. Age-wise, Jessamine had been the earliest of her siblings to move out. She was a mere eighteen when she decided to branch out and get her own place, a rundown, claptrap little house she flipped and sold for a tidy profit, parlaying into her next house, and then her next. She was on her fourth house and holding because her job had become too busy for her side business of flipping. So she had contented herself with renovating and re-renovating her current space. Besides the place where she grew up, it was the longest she had lived anywhere and felt the most like home. And now it was off-limits to her because of some psycho with a sick agenda.

How could she not have heard someone standing beside her while she slept? She had always considered herself a light sleeper, and she was accustomed to every noise in her house. In fact, her bedroom floor squeaked unless one knew exactly where to step to avoid the sagging board. Had her stalker known about the board? If so, how many times had he been in her house to learn its secrets?

She was trying hard not to give in to fear, but it wasn't easy. Not only were the local police worried about the situation, but the FBI had been brought in, at the insistence of the home and garden channel. Since it wasn't a federal crime, they were there on a consultant basis, but still. It felt to Jessamine like she had entered a wormhole and was now on a different TV show, perhaps an episode of some sort of grisly crime drama. Every time she thought of the picture, she shuddered.

Even though she was skittish, she wasn't yet ready for the private security everyone else seemed insistent on. "I'm staying at my parents for a while. Isn't that enough?" she asked the police detective in charge of the case.

"Only if you plan to be there all the time and never leave until we get this resolved," he said. "But we all know that's not possible You're a public persona now. You're going to go out and about a lot. Having a bodyguard will allow you to do that without worrying about your safety. It will be his job to worry about your safety."

"Why does it have to be a man?" Jessamine asked. "Couldn't we find a woman to guard me?"

The detective had looked at her like she lost her mind. Apparently the battle of the sexes had been fought and lost in their corner of Kentucky.

"I don't know a woman who does that. If that's what you're into, see if you can find someone," he said.

"The Queen of England has female bodyguards on her staff," she informed him, feeling slightly miffed. Seeing as how she did a job that was predominantly performed by males, she was a tad sensitive on the subject of gender stereotypes.

"See if you can get one of them to come here," the detective told her. "In the meantime, we'll go with our guy."

"Who is your guy?" she asked.

"He's a qualified professional," the detective said.

"But…" Jessamine began, but he interrupted her.

"It's all set up," he assured her, and now it was time for the meeting. Jessamine, her producer, and the detective sat in a room at the police station, waiting for her new bodyguard to show up.

"He's late," Jessamine said. Punctuality was a virtue, and it annoyed her when so-called professionals were late.

"He had a scheduling conflict. He assured me he'll be here soon," the detective told her. "Have you been able to think of anything we haven't gone over?"

"Nothing," Jessamine told him regretfully. With so little information to go on, she felt the burden of investigation was on her and her memory for possible clues. "Nothing suspicious has happened lately, besides the text I already gave you. I haven't noticed anything unusual in or around my house, I haven't sensed that I was being followed, nothing."

"There were no signs of forced entry, as we stated, and no hidden cameras at your house, at least none we've been able to find," the detective said.

"The studio has received no unusual communication, either electronically or through snail mail regarding any of the Samperis," the producer, a guy named Brett, interjected.

"The FBI is checking databases to see if it fits the profile of any other stalkers they have on file but so far they've had nothing relevant to add," Detective Harris said, his tone a bit resentful. It was clear to Jessamine that he took the FBI's involvement as a personal insult. As for her, she felt the entire investigation was hopeless. Besides the untraceable pictures with no fingerprints, they had zero evidence to go on. The stalker could be anyone, anywhere. A more likely and preferable scenario, at least to her, was that he had done what he set out to do by shaking her up and making her afraid. Now he would likely disappear and go somewhere else.

"Don't you think it's probably over?" she asked. "If he had wanted to harm me, he obviously could have while he was in my house. The fact that he didn't seems to indicate he merely wanted to scare me."

"Or it was the first move in what he's hoping will be a long game. It's a crapshoot at this point. Basically we need to wait a bit and see what his next move is," Detective Harris said. "In the meantime, we'll all rest easier if you have someone looking out for you."

"It feels like a bit of overkill to hire a bodyguard," Jessamine said.

"Please don't say kill," Brett said, grimacing. "It would be incredibly bad PR for the show if something happened to you on our watch."

"It wouldn't be great PR for our department, either," Detective Harris agreed.

"I'll try hard not to get murdered, then," Jessamine told them. "I would hate to make either of you look bad."

The detective grinned. "With that kind of morbid sense of humor, you could be a cop." Someone knocked on the door, and he stood to answer. "Thanks for coming," he said, shaking hands with whomever was at the door. He stood directly in front of Jessamine, blocking the view, but when she saw who was at the door, she stood and smacked her palm on the table.

"Nope."

"Hear him out," Detective Harris said.

Jessamine headed for the door, but the detective blocked her. "Jessamine, Milo told me you might not be happy about his appearance, but you should know he's all that's available, unless you want us to send for one of the big firms in the city. And that could take days, and we won't know if we can trust him."

"I can't trust him," she said, pointing to Milo.

"Could you give us a few minutes alone?" Milo asked.

"No," Jessamine said, but no one seemed to be listening to her anymore because Detective Harris and Brett stood and filed out of the room. Jessamine started to follow them, but Milo grabbed the back of her shirt to hold her back. She spun on him, and he dropped it, putting his hands in the air.

"Easy, I only want to talk to you, I swear," he said in the tone of someone approaching an injured grizzly.

"You cannot guard me," she said.

"Hear me out," he said.

She shook her head.

"I'm not married," he said, ignoring her objections as he eased in front of the door, physically blocking her escape path.

She cocked her head at him and scowled. "That's not what you said on Sunday."

"No, that's not what the drunk man who interrupted our dance said. He thought you were my wife, remember?"

"And I asked you if you were married, and you said it was complicated. And your tan line told me you had only recently taken off a wedding ring," she said.

"Okay, Nancy Drew, you're right on some counts. I had only taken off my wedding ring the night before the wedding rehearsal. But I hadn't been married for eighteen months," he said.

"You were divorced or separated eighteen months ago and it took you that long to take off your ring?" she asked.

"No, I was widowed. My wife died a year and a half ago," he said.

She blinked a few times. "Now I feel like a pile of garbage."

"I was hoping you would," he said, but he was grinning.

She sank back into her chair. "Why is that complicated? Why couldn't you tell me when I asked? 'Are you married? No, I'm widowed.' That's how the conversation goes."

"There are a lot of complex emotions surrounding my wife's death. I had only taken off my ring the night before, the night we met at the bar. Pardon me for not having a prepared answer on the tip of my tongue." Tentatively, he sat in the chair next to her.

"You still had no right to kiss me," she said.

"You're right, but I had to give it a go," he said. "By the way, you hit like a man. I think you loosened one of my molars."

She smiled, albeit sheepishly. "I'm sorry I hit you. That was an overreaction on my part, but I really, really, really don't like cheaters, and that's what I thought you were."

"For the record, I don't like cheaters, either. What I told you is true. I haven't cheated on anyone since some random girl I dated as a kid. I never cheated on my wife, not once, not even when we were stationed apart for months at a time."

"I'm glad to hear that. For her sake, I mean. Military wives deserve extra loyalty, I think," she said.

He nodded, but his expression clouded slightly. "So, are you going to let me work for you?"

"I don't like it," she said.

"You don't like me working for you or you don't like the thought of a bodyguard in general?" he asked.

"Both things. I don't think I need one, but the network is insisting, at least for a bit. And I like my independence. I don't want someone looking over my shoulder all the time."

"It appears someone is already looking over your shoulder all the time. Wouldn't it be comforting to have someone you know looking over the other shoulder?" he asked.

She frowned, considering, and he hastened to continue.

"And the truth is that I could use the money. I've been searching for a job since I've been out of the marines and, shockingly, there aren't a lot of openings in the corporate world for guys whose only experience is avoiding IED's while on duty in the Middle East."

"People should hire vets," she said, her frown deepening into a scowl.

"Are you going to hire a vet?" he asked.

"Ooh, you caught me. Nice trap," she said. She scratched at a stain on the cheap laminate table. "I suppose we could try it on a probationary basis."

"Good," he said. "But I have some ground rules."

She looked up. "You have ground rules? Did you not hear the part where it's probationary based on my approval?"

"Yes, but if I'm going to be in charge of keeping you safe, I need to know you're willing to follow my directions. So that's rule number one: follow my directions."

"What's rule number two?" she asked, her tone wary.

"There can be absolutely no romance between us."

She surveyed him in silence a few beats and then doubled over laughing.

CHAPTER 10

"**Y**ou're funny," she declared, wiping the moisture from beneath her eyes. "That's good. I like to surround myself with humor."

"I'm serious," he declared, causing her to laugh some more.

"Stop it, I drank a lot of coffee," she said, clutching her stomach.

"Jessamine, there's something between us," he said and she reached out a hand to clutch at him, presumably to keep herself from falling off the chair as she laughed.

"Do you have one of those magic mirrors like Snow White that tells you you're beautiful and desired by all womankind?" Jessamine asked. She reached for a tissue on the other side of the table and blew her nose.

"No, but I'm well versed in reality. Come on, tell me you didn't feel it when we were dancing," he said. "I dare you."

"Maybe there was a spark when we were dancing, but you should know that dancing often has that effect on me, and it's always temporary," she said, still smiling.

"Good because I'm serious. No romance while I'm on the job. I need to concentrate."

She sputtered, pressed her hand to her mouth, and nodded.

"It's a good thing for you my temper has a high threshold," he said. "Otherwise I might become enraged at your obvious mocking denial."

"I should be writing this stuff down in case Seasonal Affective Disorder hits hard this winter," she said. "If I call you up sometime in February and ask you to tell me not to fall in love with you, will you promise not to be offended?"

"Yes. Also, don't fall in love with me, we don't have time for it," he said, and she bent double laughing again.

"Sorry," she gasped when she could speak. "It's so funny, though. I didn't know people said things like that in real life."

"It's lucky for you that you have a charming laugh. So, do we have a deal? Are you going to let me work for you?"

"I don't suppose I have much choice," she said, dabbing at her ruined mascara. "But I have a few rules of my own."

"Something told me you would," he said.

"I need to maintain my independence. I can't feel like you're my babysitter, and I don't want to be stifled," she said.

"I get that," he said. "But think how stifled you'll feel if you're dead."

She wrinkled her nose at him.

"I'm serious, Jessamine. If you die on my watch, I will never get another job," he said.

Jessamine huffed. "I'm so sorry the prospect of my demise would inconvenience so many people financially."

"Plus I'd miss your pretty face," he added.

She rolled her eyes. "So what happens next?"

"Nothing. You go on about your business while I hover in the shadows behind you. But I want you to let me know if anything unusual happens, even if it seems insignificant. Don't discount your gut."

"Basically you're going to follow me around everywhere I go," she clarified.

"That's correct," he said. "Do what you do and I'll be in the background."

A slow smile spread across her face.

"What's that sexy, yet slightly chilling smile for?" he asked.

"I'm picturing you trying to keep up with me," she said.

"I've been in some of the worst combat situations in the world. I think I can handle following a designer for a few days," he said. "Deal?"

"All right, I guess we have a deal. See you bright and early tomorrow morning. Actually, I'll see you earlier because our day will begin before the sun," she stood to go, but he held her back.

"What's this tomorrow business? We still have half a day left. What about tonight?" he asked.

"I have plans tonight," she said.

"See, that's kind of what I'm here for, to tag along in the background of your plans."

"Hmm, how can I say this politely? No." She stood to go, but once again he hailed her back.

"Maybe you don't take this seriously, but I do. The job starts now. Where you go, I go."

"I'm going on a date," she said.

"Whoa, no one mentioned a man in the picture."

"Is that a problem?" she asked. "Because I thought you said, how was it, I am absolutely not allowed to fall in love with you." She allowed a small snicker before smoothing her expression.

"It's not that, although I do so appreciate the sneering sarcasm. Feels good. My point is that a male companion should have been the first place the police checked," he said.

"He's fine, it's not him," Jessamine said.

"How do you know?" he asked.

"Because I know."

"Still, I would feel better if I went with you and checked out the situation for myself."

"Absolutely not, end of discussion." She stood to go. He stood to block her path.

"I will stand in the background. You won't know I'm there. I'll serenade you, if you like, mariachi style."

"Well, the offer keeps getting better and better, but no," she said.

"I would feel better if I could go and meet this guy and make sure he's on the up and up," Milo said.

"He's on the up and up," Jessamine assured him.

"How do you know? Did anyone run a background check on him?" he asked.

"Yes."

"Why didn't they mention it to me?" he asked.

"Because it wasn't done by the local cops," she said.

"The FBI already cleared this guy?" he asked.

"Yes, the FBI and Congress. He's a federal judge. And he has his own security. So thanks for the offer to intrude awkwardly on my date, but it's covered. I'll see you in the morning." This time when she sidestepped him, he had no reason to call her back, but he wanted to. She had a date? With a federal judge? Was he a boyfriend? Were they serious?

She's a client, only a client. Don't get involved. Keep your wits about you. He gave himself the pep talk as he left the room and headed for the exit. Then he saw her standing at the opposite end of the hallway. She was talking on her phone, her face animated, her expressive hands moving despite the fact that the other person couldn't see her. Her face lit with a laugh, and Milo's heart stopped before freewheeling around his chest. Without a doubt, she was the most intriguing, attractive woman he had ever met, and he had purposefully placed her off limits. *This is going to go well. Good job, Milo, you've done it again.* Sighing, he braced himself for the coming days.

CHAPTER 11

Milo had been a marine for almost fifteen years. For all of that time, the country had been at war. He saw more combat than most people should see in a lifetime. There had been days when he went without sleep, times when he thought it was his last moment, and moments when he felt like giving in. He wasn't about to say tailing Jessamine Samperi was anything like that, but it was harder than he thought it would be.

In the first place, the woman never seemed to need sleep. Since leaving the military, Milo had slumped into bad habits, sometimes sleeping in until after nine. Even he was appalled by his laziness some days. But on the first day of guarding Jessamine, he rolled out of bed at four in the morning, stumbled to the shower, downed a quart of coffee, and went to pick her up at her parents' house. She, of course, was not only wide awake and stunning, but waiting on him with an impatient tap of her foot.

"You're late, Eliopoulos," she chastised.

"By thirty seconds, Samperi," he returned, stifling a yawn.

She "tsk'd" as she passed by him, and he found himself smiling at her retreating backside as he trailed after her. "My mom sent you this."

He wasn't sure she was talking to him. Her head was bent over her ever-present phone, her thumbs tapping out a message at ridiculous speed. If the designer thing didn't work out, she had a great future as a court reporter. But then she handed him a little white bag and he realized the comment had, in fact, been directed his way.

"What is it?" he asked as he opened the package and looked inside.

"Biscotti," she said distractedly, her eyes never leaving her phone.

"I love her," Milo said. His stomach growled. Four in the morning hadn't seemed like a good time for food, but after so much coffee, he found he was starving. He ate two of the biscotti before attempting to talk again. "How was your date?"

"The man himself or the event?" she asked, eyes still on the phone.

"Both."

"Charming, in both cases," she replied.

Milo scowled at the dawning horizon. What did that mean? He chanced a glance at Jessamine and had to force his eyes back to the road. She was like a painting; he could stare at her for hours. It wasn't only that she was beautiful, it was more. There was something about her that drew him in. She was like a puzzle he wanted to solve. What made her tick? What was she thinking? What drove her so relentlessly? He was beginning to discover what made her laugh, but what made her sad?

"Eyes on the road, driver," she said, and his attention snapped to the forefront.

"There's no traffic," he told her.

"There are trees, and I'd prefer not to end up wrapped around one," she said.

"Diva," he breathed and she reached over the seat and poked him, all without removing her eyes from the phone.

"Who could you possibly be texting at five in the morning?" he asked.

"My aunt."

"Is your aunt an insomniac or crazy early riser?" he asked.

"Neither, she lives in Italy. It's eleven there," she said.

"Have you ever been?" he asked.

"No, have you ever been to Greece?" she asked.

"Yes," he said, and she finally looked up.

"How was it?" Her eyes were alight with curiosity, and he was once again in danger of driving off the road. He forced himself to stare forward as he answered.

"As amazing as you'd imagine. How come you've never been to Italy if you have family there?"

"Never had the time," she said, sounding wistful.

"Um, you're self-employed. Make the time," he said.

"It's not that simple."

"Of course it is," he argued.

She reached across the seat again and began absently feeling his bicep.

"Now what are you doing?" he asked.

"Looking for your off switch," she said.

"I don't have one," he said.

"I was afraid of that. Note to self: bring earbuds tomorrow," she said.

"Ha, ha, adorable," he said with full sarcasm as he reached across the seat and squeezed her knee.

She jumped and smacked his hand away. "No touchie."

"Because you're ticklish or because it makes it harder for you to keep your hands off me?" he asked.

"Because you're driving, and I don't want your biscotti-laden fingers on my white linen pants," she said.

"High maintenance much?" He chanced another glance at her and saw her smiling slightly as she continued to text. "Do you always dress this nicely to go to work, or is that for my benefit?"

"Yes, Milo, it's all about you. Normally I wear torn rags when I'm going to appear on television, but this morning I thought, 'You know what, let's look good for the chauffer.'"

"I'm so much more than your chauffer," he said.

"Says the man who's driving me to work," she said.

"If Miss Daisy was this mouthy, I think Morgan Freeman would have dumped her on the side of the road," Milo said.

"Miss Daisy was a southern lady. She was plenty mouthy," Jessamine argued.

"Are you still texting your aunt?" he asked.

"No, Ma, I'm texting a supplier in New York," she said. "And, yes, he's up at five and ready to work. Or maybe he never went to sleep. Not sure."

"When do you sleep? You do sleep, don't you?" he asked.

"Are you implying I'm a vampire?" she asked.

"I'm not implying anything. I'm flat out saying you seem to have a super-human energy level," he said.

"I sleep, but I'm one of those people who doesn't need a lot. Four hours, and I'm good."

"Me, too," he said. "Four hours, times two, plus three, and I'm good to go."

"How did you survive the military?" she asked.

"I survived because I had to, but now that I'm out, I'm making up for lost time. Sleep, good."

"Espresso, good," she said, taking a sip from her insulated travel mug.

They arrived at the studio in Lexington where she shot a weekly television spot on the local morning program. After that they drove back home where she went to work on a project with her brothers for the next six hours. The television crews were filming there, too. They told Milo they would edit him out of any shots, but he did his best to stay in the background anyway. It was fun to watch the Samperis work. He hadn't seen the show, first because he hadn't known it existed until a few days ago and then because he didn't have cable or fast enough internet to stream the show.

The way they interacted with Jessamine was most fascinating to him. The brothers shared an interesting combination of frustration and deference toward their only sister. It was clear they loved her, perhaps even adored and cherished her. But it was also clear she drove them all crazy with her insistence on being in control of every aspect of the design. Currently she and Joe were locked in an unending feud over the placement of a beam.

"You said we weren't taking out the supports on this one," Joe reminded her, yelling.

"I changed my mind," Jessamine yelled.

"Why do you always change your mind in the middle? Why can't you change it in the beginning?" he yelled.

"It's better than changing it at the end," she yelled.

"You've done that, too," he yelled.

"By taking out the supports and putting in the beam, we'll add space and openness to the kitchen, not to mention a floor to ceiling pantry cabinet," Jessamine yelled.

"Along with fifteen thousand dollars to the budget," Joe yelled.

"I'll take it from somewhere else," Jessamine yelled.

"No, you won't," Joe yelled. "You never do."

"And yet it always turns out okay," she said, smiling as she sensed he was about to give in.

He rolled his eyes. She jumped on his back and kissed his cheek, hugging him. "Get off, you monkey," he groused, but he was smiling. Ten minutes later, the crew began taking out the supports.

Meanwhile, Milo's stomach growled. It was one in the afternoon. He hadn't eaten since Mrs. Samperi's biscotti eight hours ago. He tapped Jessamine's shoulder and touched his watch. "Lunch?"

"I don't usually eat lunch," she said, distracted.

"I do," he said.

"Go ahead," she said, and then she actually shooed him away with her fingers.

"I can't leave you here," he said.

"I'm with my brothers; I'm fine," she assured him.

"Oh, okay. Which one of your brothers is carrying a gun?" he asked.

She finally looked up from her sketchbook. "None. Why would they?"

With effort, he refrained from rolling his eyes. "I'm getting lunch, and you're coming with me."

"I'm busy," she said.

"And I'm hungry. Believe me when I tell you mine wins, so you can either come willingly, or I'll carry you to the car," he said.

She blew out a frustrated breath. "Men and their stomachs."

"Women and their…" he gave her the once over, looking for a flaw. "Just get in the car."

With a last huff, she set down her sketchbook and marched toward the car. Behind her back, Moss gave Milo a smile and a thumb's up, presumably because he'd gotten Jessamine to do something she wasn't willing to do. Even after knowing her only a few days, he realized how miraculous that was.

As a deference to her busyness, he drove through a restaurant so they could return quickly to her worksite.

"Are you really armed?" she asked.

He moved aside his jacket to show her his holster.

"Would you actually use it?" she asked.

"To protect someone? In a heartbeat," he said. "There's a lot of bad in the world, Jess." She ordered a salad. He handed it to her before taking his massive double burger meal. His stomach felt so empty he could barely contain himself from gnawing through the wrapper. "Why don't you eat?"

"I do eat, a lot. I mean, you've met my mother. But I get sort of absorbed in my work and don't like to stop," she said.

Her whole work ethic was worrisome to him. Besides her family, she seemed to have no life outside her job. Granted, her job seemed pretty awesome and she loved it, but still. She ate, slept, and breathed work. And the phone was like another appendage. But none of these things were his business. Knowing her as he was beginning to, she definitely wouldn't appreciate his opinion on the subject.

"How's your salad?" he asked and she relaxed, as if she had been waiting for a rebuke about her work style. She opened the clamshell containing her salad and sniffed before closing it again.

"Eh, needs garlic," she noted.

"I take it you won't be seeing the federal judge anytime again soon," he said.

"Why?"

"Because garlic," he said.

"If garlic deterred people from romance, we Italians would have died out centuries ago," she said. "Besides, there's a trick to it."

"What's that? Consume an entire mint plant after dinner?"

"No, if both people eat garlic, you cancel each other out," she said.

"Are you telling me you can only be with a man if he likes garlic?" he asked.

"Among other things," she said.

"What things?" he asked.

"Is that pertinent to our working relationship, driver?" she asked.

"Yes. Like all good bodyguards, I need to know the dating requirements of my clients. Did Kevin Costner and Whitney Houston teach you nothing?" he asked.

"My biggest takeaway from that movie is that Dolly Parton is a songwriting genius."

"What does Dolly Parton have to do with anything?" he asked.

"She wrote the song Whitney Houston sang at the end," she said.

"I didn't know that. Wow, that's a good song."

"That's because she's a genius and, despite the fact that Whitney was supernaturally gifted, I like Dolly's version better. It's so real, so relatable," Jessamine said. They arrived back at the worksite, but she made no move to get out of the car. Instead she opened her salad and began to eat. Following her lead, Milo opened his sandwich and tried not to attack it like a feral dog on road kill, as his empty stomach was urging him to do. They finished and sat in comfortable silence a few minutes. Milo wondered what she was thinking but lacked the courage to ask. It wasn't like him to be self-conscious, but he had never been in his current position before—widowed and jobless. He was suddenly keenly aware of the differences between them. Jessamine was a woman who had her life together. She needed a man who could say the same. At the moment, that wasn't him.

Eventually she returned to the job and worked five hours longer. When she was finished, Milo would never admit how much he hoped the day was over. It had been almost fourteen hours and he was hungry again.

"What's next?" he asked with entirely fake enthusiasm he hoped she wouldn't detect.

"Supper," she said.

"At your mom's?" he asked hopefully.

"At a restaurant with a client. It's a business meeting," she said.

"Super," he exclaimed, showing all his teeth when he smiled.

Jessamine wasn't fooled. "Are you regretting taking this job yet?"

"Nope," he said, and that was true. Being tired wasn't enough of a reason to quit. He had missed working; he *liked* working. The problem was that his degree and training weren't applicable to everything. He wanted a job that suited him, and it was taking time to find the right fit.

The restaurant was a swanky steakhouse named Patrino's. Milo couldn't help but chuckle a bit when he saw it.

"Good memories of this place?" Jessamine asked.

"The best," Milo said, but he didn't elaborate.

She glanced at him curiously but didn't press him on it. "This meeting might take a while. The client is particularly particular," she warned.

"I've got all night," he said.

"You're being awfully patient and agreeable," she noted.

"I *am* patient and agreeable," he said.

"That makes one of us," she said. "I have zero patience and my senior superlative was almost 'most irritable' before the staff advisor made them change it."

He laughed. "You think I'm joking, but I'm not," she said.

"I don't think you're joking. I think you're…Anyway, we should probably get inside. Something tells me whoever you're meeting wouldn't like it if you're late."

"He'll hate it; that's why I'm making him wait," she said.

"Earlier today you freaked out because I was thirty seconds late. Now you're purposely being late. I'm so confused right now," he said.

"Power," she explained. "He wants it, but I've got it, and I don't intend to give it up."

"You're all kinds of fascinating," Milo said.

"It's nice you think so," Jessamine said, sounding sincere. She checked the time on her phone. "I think we've made him wait long enough. Ready?"

"I'm only here to hover in the background. Are you ready?" He returned.

"Always," she replied and, with head high and heels clicking, walked to the restaurant.

CHAPTER 12

Milo was an affable guy. There weren't many people he genuinely disliked, but Jessamine's client was now on his list. First off, he was weird. He had the pale, boneless appearance of someone who was regularly drained of blood. His face and skin were the same dull grayish beige of his suit. Even his lips were pale. Initially, Milo thought he was sick and felt bad about all the unkind, judgmental thoughts running through his head. Then he realized the lack of color had nothing to do with illness and everything to do with temperament. The man was so unlikeable he somehow ended up looking as bad as he was.

The second thing Milo noticed was the man's over-the-top snobbery. Traveling the world had made Milo appreciate America's classless society, but apparently this man hadn't gotten the message because he looked Milo up and down and immediately dismissed him as the help.

"You're late," were the man's first words to Jessamine. Milo bristled at his proprietary tone, but Jessamine smiled and waved her hand dismissively.

"You know how these things go." There were only two chairs at the table. Jessamine made eye contact with the waiter who scurried to provide another. Jessamine sat, and Milo took the seat to her left.

"Who is this and why is he here?" the man asked, not trying to cover his sneer as he stared at Milo.

"This is my assistant, Milo. Milo, this is my client, Hans Gelding."

"I was under the impression you worked alone," Hans said, ignoring Milo's nod and outstretched hand.

"Professionally, yes. Milo is helping me with some personal matters," Jessamine said.

"Then I'd like him to leave. This is a private meeting," Hans said.

Milo opened his mouth to intervene, but there was no need. The atmosphere turned chilly, and Jessamine spoke. "If Milo leaves, then I leave with him." She put her hand on her purse and started to rise. With a huff, Hans hailed her back.

"He can stay, but it may become necessary to have him sign a non-disclosure agreement," Hans said, narrowing his eyes at Milo who hid his smile in return. Was this guy for real? Like Milo was going to go sell Jessamine's designs to the highest bidder the moment Hans turned around?

"He's trustworthy," Jessamine said, patting his knee.

A bud of warmth blossomed in Milo's chest and spread outward. She trusted him. She had said it for the creepy client, but he'd take it. And she had touched him of her own volition. He wanted to take the hand that had been on his knee, twine their fingers together, and use it to draw her out of the room and away from the colorless man. Even his eyes were a lifeless shade of amber. It was like staring at a python.

The waitress arrived and they ordered. Milo wanted to order a steak, but he wasn't certain if he should. He didn't want to be that guy who took advantage of the company's dime. Jessamine seemed to sense his dilemma as he stared at the menu.

"It's a steakhouse, Eliopoulos," she whispered, flipping his menu from the sandwiches back to the steaks.

Hans ordered as badly as he did everything else. "There will be exactly three inches of pink in the center of my steak. Anything more or less and I will send it back. I want horseradish on the side, not the disgusting mayonnaise concoction, but actual horseradish. If the restaurant doesn't keep it in stock, have someone go buy it for me. These carrots, are they organic?"

"I'll have to check on that," the flustered waitress replied.

Hans sighed as if she had told him his suspicious mole was cancerous and he had three months to live.

Jessamine ordered a steak with baked potato and salad, and Milo had the same. "And I want exactly three inches of sour cream on the potato, or I'm sending it back," he added with a wink for the waitress that made her smile and blush. She was a cute kid, probably barely eighteen, and definitely not deserving of a customer like Hans. "She tips well," he added in a whisper, nodding at Jessamine.

"It's true, I do," Jessamine said, smiling as she handed over her menu.

"How hard is it to wait tables?" Hans demanded when the waitress was still in earshot.

"Really hard," Milo snapped. It was the first he'd spoken, besides placing his order.

"I suppose you'd know," Hans said, eyeing Milo with extra disdain.

"My mom was a waitress in Brooklyn before she had kids," Jessamine added. "She still talks about how difficult and exhausting it was."

"I suppose you're right," Hans agreed. "Where would we be without the servant classes?" He tipped his cup to Milo, as if indicating he was still part of the servant class. It took everything in Milo not to laugh. There was a time, many years ago when he was a kid, that Milo would have been tempted to punch him in the face. But time, age, life, maturity, and more than a decade in the military had changed all that. He knew who he was; he had no need to prove it to Hans. Now he didn't even reply. He sat back with an amused smile and, when his meal arrived, enjoyed it completely. He hadn't had a good steak in ages, and this one was done to perfection, as were the potato and salad.

"Let's get started, shall we?" Hans said. Of course he was the kind of man who chewed with his mouth open, giving them all a nice view of his masticated steak and potato. "I've taken the liberty of putting together a collage of what I have in mind for my chateau."

He withdrew a portfolio and set it on the table between him and Jessamine. Jessamine browsed through his ideas, giving each one serious regard as he droned on an on about the absolute precision and perfection of his ideal house. Milo loved watching her work, he realized. Her big eyes were serious and vivid. He could almost imagine the mental pictures swirling in her head. She was all in, totally absorbed in her internal monologue. Based on what Hans was saying, the account had to be huge and lucrative. He was describing a house the size and scale of a small institution with custom everything that would have to be carved into the side of a remote stone hillside. It was exactly the sort of thing the Samperis excelled at, and it would be great for the show, as would Hans. His over-the-top persona was the stuff of a television producer's dreams.

"Your project looks intriguing," Jessamine said. Hans puffed up as if she'd patted his head instead of his ego. "I'm sorry to say I don't think we'll be able to do it."

"Why not?" Hans demanded.

"I don't think it's the right fit for us," Jessamine said. "I'd be happy to refer you to someone else, someone capable and trustworthy."

"But they won't be on TV, will they?" Hans demanded.

"Not to my knowledge, but not all of our projects make it on television. That process is up to the producers, not us. Even if we took you on, there would be no guarantee of appearing on television," Jessamine said.

"It's not about TV anyway," he said, an obvious lie. The man was so hungry for power, fame, and recognition he was practically oozing with it. "It's about hiring the best, and you're the best."

"I appreciate that, but this isn't what I do. You already have the vision of what you want. All you need is someone to carry it out," Jessamine said.

"I want that to be you," Hans said, a hard edge to his tone.

"It won't be," Jessamine said, steel in her voice, too. So far it had all been words, but then Hans reached forward and wrapped his icy fingers around her bicep, squeezing hard. Before he got a word out, Milo was across the table with his hand on Hans's throat.

"Let. Her. Go," Milo demanded. Hans dropped Jessamine's arm, and Milo released his grip, too. The restaurant had come to a stand still and all eyes were on them. "Take your stuff and go."

Hans didn't argue. He was the type of bully who was only brave until someone bigger and scarier came along. Now that Milo was a large and looming threat—with a gun, no less—he was ready to tuck his tail and run home to Mama. Without a word, he gathered his portfolio, but after he stood, he spoke again.

"You'll be hearing from my lawyer."

"Good. Her lawyer can tell you the meaning of assault," Milo said. He flicked his fingers toward the exit. Scowling, Hans turned and walked away. Milo waited until he was gone to sit down. "Are you okay?" he asked Jessamine.

"I'm fine," she assured him. "Guys like him are nothing new."

"Are you trying to tell me someone has manhandled you like that before?" Milo demanded.

"I work with men for a living. Most of them are great, wonderful guys. Over the years there have been a few who weren't so great. But the beauty of having four brothers is that I'm pretty good at taking care of myself and, when I'm not, my brothers are more than willing to take charge," she said. She patted his knee again. "Thanks for doing that. It saved me the trouble of going nuclear on him."

He couldn't help himself, this time he captured her hand and held on. "I kind of wanted to send his teeth down his throat."

"I kind of wanted that, too," Jessamine said, giving his hand a squeeze. "Are you doing all right?" Her hand pressed to his heart, presumably checking its rate. After his PTSD display with the gunshots on Sunday, he couldn't blame her for her concern.

"I'm fine," he assured her. He covered the hand on his heart so that now both their hands were touching. In the middle of a crowded restaurant. With everyone still watching them. Jessamine withdrew her hands and sat back. Milo felt cold at the sudden withdrawal, but he didn't reach for her. He wanted to, but he refrained. *Focus, focus, focus,* he reminded himself.

"Milo!" A man came from the kitchen, calling his name. Milo stood.

"Mr. Patrino." The two men hugged before bestowing their attention on Jessamine. "This is Jessamine Samperi."

"I know Jessamine," Mr. Patrino said. "I didn't know you knew Milo."

"I didn't know *you* knew Milo," Jessamine said.

"This kid," Mr. Patrino said, shaking his head. "I hired him as a busboy, but he charmed the customers so well I had to make him a waiter. I think you still hold the record for most tips received in a night."

"Bachelorette party," Milo explained with an eyebrow wag for Jessamine's benefit.

With effort, she refrained from rolling her eyes. Having known how he was in high school, she could well imagine how easily he had charmed a bridal party out of their money.

"It's been so long," Mr. Patrino continued. "I thought you were in the army."

"The marines," Milo corrected. "I was, but I'm out now."

"And dating Jessamine," Mr. Patrino said. "If I had known you were home, I would have tried to set you up. You two are perfect for each other."

Milo expected Jessamine to argue. When she didn't, he inserted his own question. "How do you two know each other?"

"Marie and my wife play cards together, every Tuesday night for the last eighteen years," Mr. Patrino explained. He looked between them with a happy smile. "Jessamine and Milo. This makes my old heart so happy."

Milo waited for Jessamine to contradict, but she merely gave Mr. Patrino a gentle smile and patted his arm. They said their goodbyes and he held the door for her.

"It's easier to let him live with his delusions, you know?" Jessamine commented once they were tucked into the car. "People are going to believe what they want to about us. Small town living, and all that."

"Right, right," Milo agreed. Secretly he wondered if he was one of the people having delusions. He couldn't stop believing that somehow they would work out and, like Mr. Patrino, he didn't want his bubble to be burst. "So, what's next?"

"Home, James," she declared.

"Already?" he said, but what he actually wanted to say was *finally*. It had been a sixteen-hour day, and he was exhausted.

"Don't be too disappointed. In eight hours, we'll do it all again," she said.

They made the drive to her house in comfortable silence. He expected her to protest when he walked her to the door, but she didn't. They faced each other like the end of a date instead of a long day of work.

"Call if you need anything, if anything feels off, if you're suspicious," he said.

"What if I just want to talk?" she asked.

"That, too," he said, ridiculously hopeful she meant it, even though by her smile he knew she was teasing.

"I'll be fine," she assured him. "Will you? You look like you're about to fall over."

"Me? I have the energy of a spring lamb. I'm going to go home, lift weights, run a few miles, have some target practice, do laundry, maybe paint a picture, train for a triathlon. Or I'll curl up in a ball in the back seat of my car and sleep in your driveway like a stray cat. It's really a tossup."

She laughed, and his heart turned over. He was in serious trouble when it came to her. She had him wrapped, and they hadn't even had an actual date or shared a real kiss. And he owed her a thousand dollars. And he had no job. And his personal life was a mess. And someone was stalking her.

"You should probably take off before..." Her mother opened the door and poked her head out before Jessamine could complete the sentence.

"Milo, how nice to see you, dear. I just took some cannoli out of the fryer. Would you like to come in? Jessamine, invite your friend inside."

"Ma," Jessamine said, sounding uncharacteristically embarrassed.

Milo smiled. "I would love to, Mrs. Samperi, really, but I need to stop by and see my mother before I go home. Thank you so much for the invitation."

"Rain check," Mrs. Samperi said.

"Ma," Jessamine snapped again.

"What does that have to do with you, little miss?" Mrs. Samperi demanded. "Isn't it possible I enjoy Milo's company? Look at that pretty face, and such a good eater." She held Milo's chin in her hand and gave it an approving pat before turning and disappearing back inside.

"I'm so sorry," Jessamine said. It was hard to tell in the dim porch light, but she appeared to be blushing. He touched her cheek and found it warm.

"I really like your family," he said.

"They don't overwhelm, terrify, and embarrass you?" she said.

"Not even a little." His hand was still on her cheek. He dropped it quickly to his side and took a step back. "Same time tomorrow. I'll be the one with toothpicks propping my eyes open."

Jessamine closed the distance between them again and kissed his cheek. "Goodnight, Milo."

Milo squeezed his eyes shut, willing his hands to stay at his sides so they didn't reach for her like they wanted. He sealed his lips together, refusing to let them stray to her mouth. "Goodnight, Jess." His voice was croaky, but she didn't comment. "I'm going to sweep the perimeter before I leave. Tell your father not to shoot me if he sees someone outside the window." Mr. Samperi, as it turned out, *did* have a gun and knew how to use it. After arriving in Kentucky he had learned to hunt, and each year took part in a charity pheasant hunt.

"Will do," Jessamine promised. He waited for her to go inside and close the door. Only after the bolt slid did he turn and release the breath he'd been holding. One day down and hopefully only a few more to go. Surely they would catch her stalker soon, wouldn't they? He couldn't guard her forever, denying himself the opportunity to flirt with her, to touch her or kiss her.

On the other hand, maybe the forced waiting was a good thing. Milo was in no condition to start a romance with anyone, least of all a woman like Jessamine Samperi. He was still healing, still recovering, still getting his life together. Maybe by the time her stalker was found, he'd have everything figured out. He'd have a job and his personal life wouldn't be such a train wreck. It was unlikely, but he'd always believed in miracles. And to be with a woman like Jessamine Samperi, he would definitely need divine intervention.

CHAPTER 13

For the next four days, life was on repeat. Up at five in the morning, work all day, pause for lunch, work through supper, and say goodnight. The only difference was that Mrs. Samperi packed a lunch for Milo, probably at Jessamine's request so he wouldn't badger her to stop working. To say she loved her job would be an understatement. The woman lived for her career. Milo enjoyed working; Jessamine needed work like she needed oxygen. He would have worried about her except she seemed to be having so much fun.

After the first day when everything was new and interesting, Milo became bored. There was only so much standing or watching or checking the perimeter he could do in a day. Eventually he sat and watched and had to force his mind away from daydreams. *Focus, focus, focus,* he constantly reminded himself. In order to try and concentrate on his job, he began to think of who might be Jessamine's stalker. The most obvious suspect was someone with direct access to her. She was smart about her privacy, only giving out her phone number to a select few trusted friends and family. Her address was hidden beneath layers of legal bureaucracy. Milo spent a long time watching her brothers and their interaction with their sister. With the possible exception of Moss, none of them enjoyed the television show as much as she did.

Joe especially made no secret of his disdain for the venture, appearing on camera far less than anyone else. Could one of her brothers be stalking her out of jealousy or resentment? Having known Joe and Benny for most of his life, it was hard for Milo to imagine such a scenario.

But he had to be impartial, and so he tried to view them as if he were a stranger. The three younger brothers were either newlyweds or soon-to-be married. They were in their own little worlds. Joe had been married for two decades and, judging by the ginger way everyone tiptoed around the subject, he and Peaches seemed to be having a rough patch. If anyone in the family was Jessamine's stalker, Joe would be the perfect suspect—unhappy, resentful, frustrated. But no matter how many times Milo tried, he couldn't make it stick. Joe was so *nice*. Despite the fact that having a film crew on hand wasn't his first choice, he was doing it because Jessamine wanted it. That was the sort of man he was, the kind who put the needs of others ahead of himself. How could a guy like that do something as evil as terrify his little sister? He couldn't. After viewing each one through an objective lens, Milo discounted the brothers as suspects.

Next he turned his attention to the camera crew and producer. They spent a lot of time with the Samperis. A few of the men were single and, maybe due to his heightened awareness of her, Milo thought some showed a bit too much vested interest in Jessamine. The camera loved her, but was that because the cameras spent so much time trained on her? The crew remained on his suspect list, even after careful analysis and speculation.

Or maybe it was some crazy, random person who had meticulously researched her, becoming an invisible part of her life, working in the shadows. However he spun it, he had no answers, and the lack frustrated him. How long could they go on this way? Jessamine was already chafing at the constraints on her life. She didn't like living with her parents, and she didn't like having Milo as a babysitter everywhere she went. Despite how unobtrusive he tried to be, the fact that he was always there grated on her desperate need for independence.

On the fifth day, the police detective called a meeting. "Do you think this is it?" Jessamine asked Milo, her tone hopeful. "Do you think it's over and they caught him?"

"I don't know," Milo said. He didn't want to disappoint her, but he wasn't as optimistic as she was. They drove to the station in silence. The quiet between them was always comfortable, and that bothered Milo. He was almost positive he was being friendzoned. After so much time spent together the last few days, all the signs were there. Jessamine found him attractive, yes, but they weren't moving forward. They were hovering somewhere between co-workers and pals and not nearly as close to romance as he wanted. *You told her it wasn't going to happen,* he reminded himself. That part was true, but he had secretly hoped she would protest or put up more of a struggle about it. Instead she seemed happy to write him off, to put him in the buddy category where she kept everyone else. Worse, maybe she was even beginning to view him like one of her brothers. If that happened, it might be the death knell from which he would never recover. But what could he do to stop it? He was stuck in limbo until her stalker was caught and he was off the clock as her bodyguard.

At the station, the room was crowded with officers, both local and federal. It had the makings of a long meeting, and Milo regretted the copious amount of coffee he'd consumed.

"Jessamine, thank you for coming," Detective Harris said, coming forward to shake her hand and welcome her into the room. "Milo," he added with a nod.

"George," Milo said, returning his nod.

There was one open chair. Jessamine sat in it, and Milo assumed his customary space—hovering in the background behind her.

"We wanted to touch base, see where we are, go over a few things," the detective said.

"You haven't caught him yet?" Jessamine asked. The question might have seemed abrupt and accusatory, if not for the raw hope in her tone.

"We're making progress," the detective assured her. "Between us and the feds, we're going to get this figured out in no time. The feds have turned up a few profiles of celebrity stalkers we want to go over with you today. How's it going with you two?" His glance bounced worriedly between Jessamine and Milo. Last time he left them, they hadn't been on good terms.

"It's fine," Jessamine said with a dismissive wave, not even looking at Milo.

Ouch, Milo thought. He should be happy they were getting along so well, not yearning for something more.

"Good," the detective said. "Let's get started."

They went over everything again, first the local cops and then the feds. Jessamine's phone buzzed and vibrated. Her hand itched, desperate to answer it. Milo shifted from foot to foot. At last there was a break in the endless rehashing while the cops and feds talked to each other. Jessamine snatched her phone, and Milo leaned down to whisper in her ear.

"I'll be back in one minute. Do not leave this room, do not leave this chair. Yes?"

She nodded, distracted.

Milo sprinted to the bathroom and returned in record time, not even bothering to dry his hands after he washed them. He opened the door and stopped short, his heart plummeting to his shoes. Jessamine was gone.

"Where is she?" he loudly demanded. The other men came to a standstill and faced him in confusion.

"I thought she was with you," one of them said.

Milo didn't argue. He turned and erupted out of the room. "Check the bathroom," he yelled at one of the female feds. Where would Jessamine go? *To make a call.* He could practically picture her, hand pressed to her ear in the loud room, going in search of a quiet place to talk. *The stairwell.*

He ripped open the door. Adrenaline shot through his body like a tidal wave, triggering his heart into such a fast gallop that it felt in danger of flying out of his body. Jessamine was there, her body pressed against the wall and blocked by a man, his head covered by a mask, his fingers obscured by leather gloves. Milo had no idea what he was doing, only that he was touching her. He yanked the man away with such force that he tossed him down the stairs in one fluid motion. The door to the stairwell opened, and more officers tumbled through.

"There," Milo pointed down the stairs where the man was already up and running. Milo didn't care about him. He turned to face Jessamine, terrified of what he might find. Was she hurt? Was she *alive*?

Her mouth was open in an unspoken pucker of exclamation, her large eyes glazed with fear and shock. Her blouse had been shredded. Had the man been carrying a knife? Milo hadn't noticed, but everything had happened so quickly. He moved forward and inspected her for cuts, running his hands down her arms. She jumped at his touch.

"Shh, it's okay. I'm seeing if you're hurt. Did he cut you? Are you bleeding?"

She shook her head.

"My shirt, he cut my shirt. Why would he do that?" Her face was colorless. Any moment, she was going to faint. Milo took off his jacket and put it around her. He sat, pulling her down beside him. Her teeth started to chatter. He wrapped her in a tight hug. When that didn't stop her trembling, he pulled her into his lap and cradled her like a baby. She slipped her arms around his waist and pressed her face to his shoulder.

"You're okay, you're safe," Milo repeated, smoothing his hand over her crazy curls. The female fed poked her head into the hallway.

"She okay?"

"Could you get her some juice and crackers?" Milo requested.

"Not hungry," Jessamine muttered.

"It'll help with the shock. Trust me," he said. The woman returned a few minutes later with apple juice and some saltines. Milo's eyebrows rose, asking her the unspoken question. *Did they get the guy?* She shook her head before closing the door. He tamped down his frustration. He shouldn't have thrown him down the stairs. He should have tackled him and held him until someone with cuffs arrived, regardless of whether or not he had a knife. But he hadn't been thinking clearly. All he had been able to think at the time was that he needed to get the man off Jessamine, to save her, to make sure she was all right.

He bade Jessamine to take some of the food. She took a bite of the cracker and drank half the juice before setting it aside.

"Can I go home?" she asked.

"Absolutely," Milo said.

"They're not going to make me stay and do interviews and stuff?" she asked.

"I won't let them. We're going home," he assured her.

Detective Harris did try to waylay them, but Milo was having none of it.

"Neither of us saw anything. I'm taking her home, she'll talk to you later," Milo assured him, not sticking around to hear another option.

As unobtrusively as possible, he drew his weapon before they left the station. If the stalker had been bold enough to attack in broad daylight at a police station, what else would he be willing to do? Milo didn't know, but he was done taking chances.

CHAPTER 14

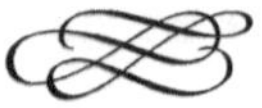

They made it to the car without interference. Milo tucked Jessamine in and slid behind the wheel, securing his weapon after locking the doors. It was more than likely the stalker knew where Jessamine was staying, but he took a roundabout way to her parents' house anyway.

Jessamine was subdued. He knew her well enough by now to understand what a bad sign that was. She wasn't the sort of person who needed to be the center of attention, but she was animated, a live wire, full of spark and energy. Now she sat staring out the window, barely blinking or breathing. Milo reached across the seat and clasped her hand, giving it a squeeze. Her fingers were cold, her body probably still in shock.

"We're almost there. I'm taking the scenic route," he explained.

"I know," she said, mouse-like. She shifted the position of their hands, clasping his between both of hers. Why was she studying his fingers so intently? Or was she? Maybe her mind was a million miles away and she had no idea what she was doing.

At last they arrived at her parents' house. Milo drew his weapon again and put his arm around her, shepherding her to the house.

Normally she would have protested that he was manhandling her. Today she let herself be led meekly to the door and stood by while he unlocked it.

"No one's home," she noted absently. Milo stood by the door a moment, letting his ears adjust to the silence of the house. It felt empty, but he would check it to be sure.

"Which room is yours?" he asked.

"Upstairs, second on the right," she said.

He clasped her hand and used it to lead her up the stairs. Once there, she sat on the bed, staring around in confusion as if she wasn't sure where she was or how she got there. If not for her suitcase on the floor, Milo might have thought he had the wrong room. He knelt in front of her, took off her shoes, and set them neatly to the side. Chafing her hands between both his, he finally spoke.

"You need to change out of these clothes. Tell me what to get, and I'll bring it."

"In my suitcase I have a pair of black yoga pants and a UK hoodie," she said. He retrieved them and handed them to her. She took them as if they were foreign objects and set them on the bed beside her.

"Do you need help?" he asked. He tried to say it neutrally, maybe even kindly, but her eyes sparked a little, the first sign of life from her since the attack.

"You'd like that, wouldn't you?" she asked.

"Incredibly much, yes," he said, grinning.

One corner of her mouth raised a fraction. "Turn around."

He complied, turning his back to her while her clothes rustled and shifted. "Okay," she said after a few minutes. He faced her again and his smile widened.

"What?" she said, a bit of the old, snappish Jess coming through.

"This is the first time I've seen you in anything but dress clothes, so I'm making a mental note to thank the guy who invented yoga pants." He reached down and pulled the covers back for her. "Lie down."

She complied with a worrisome lack of argument. He tucked the blanket around her and smoothed the wild hairs off her forehead. "Try to rest. This will all seem better when you wake up," he urged. He took a step away.

"Don't go," she pled.

He froze. "You want me to stand in here while you sleep?"

She rolled her eyes. "You're not a marine anymore. At ease, soldier." She patted the bed beside her, scooting over slightly to make room for him. Milo didn't need to be told twice. He shucked off his shoes, hung his jacket on the chair, and took off his shoulder holster, laying it gingerly on the nightstand. He crawled into the bed beside her and then, for possibly the first time in his life, he wasn't sure what to do. Did she merely want his presence to block the inevitable memories and nightmares? Was he supposed to hold her? What did she want from him?

"If you hadn't told me you'd been married, I might think you've never done this before," she said.

"It's because I was married that I don't know what to do," he admitted. "It's been a long time."

"Let me settle your anxieties: nothing's going to happen here. I just need a friend, I need a shoulder," Jessamine said.

"You're in luck, I have two." Was he relieved or disappointed? Maybe a little of both. He rolled toward her and took her in his arms, letting his embrace envelope her. "If I press my nose to your hair and inhale, it's because that's what friends do in Greek culture, so don't read anything into it." Figuring he'd bought himself some leeway, he did press his nose to her hair and inhale. She smelled even better up close than she did from far away. Jessamine must not have minded because she pressed her face to his neck, nestling it in the crook of his collarbone as if the spot had been on reserve for her. So intoxicated was he by the feel of her, the smell of her, that it took him a minute to realize she was crying.

"Jess, it's okay, it's over, you're safe," he said, his hand smoothing gently over her mane of now-tangled curls.

"I'm sorry," she said, her words muffled by his clavicle.

"You're allowed to cry," he told her.

"No, I'm sorry I left the room. You said not to, and I did it anyway. I didn't think the threat was real, I didn't believe he'd try to hurt me," she said.

He pulled away from her to see her face. "Don't think like that, don't apologize. You're a grown woman who took a phone call. You're not a child, not a prisoner. It's not your fault any more than it's my fault for having a full bladder. It's only his fault for trying to terrorize you, but we won't let him. After a little rest, you're going to be fine. You're going to bounce back, and it will be like today never happened."

She gazed up at him with sad, soulful, teary eyes. And then she kissed him. It was all wrong, of course. She was needy and a little bit panicked, but Milo didn't even consider not responding. The minute her lips touched his, he was all in. A full three minutes later, she broke away.

"I'm sorry," she breathed.

"Now why are you apologizing?" he asked. Her face was still in his hands, her lips as swollen and chafed as his felt. His thumb smoothed over her bottom lip. Her lips were beautiful, a deep ruby color and impossibly full.

"You said no kissing," she reminded him.

"Comfort kisses don't count," he told her. Nothing counted when she was the one making the moves. He had put those safeguards in place for himself, so he wouldn't overstep his bounds with her, never imagining she would be the one to kiss him first. But since she did, only a fool would say no, only a heartless robot would push her away.

"I need a mass dose of comfort," she said and kissed him again, her arms twining around his neck to pull him impossibly closer.

Milo was gone. He might have been able to pull himself back from the ledge with anyone else, but not this woman. She did something to him—she had since the moment they met. Why? He had no idea, and he didn't care. All he knew was that he didn't want whatever was happening to stop, ever.

If they hadn't been so intent on each other, they might have heard the footsteps outside, along with the door being opened. "Well, I heard you were attacked and rushed right home. Either that's Milo, or the attack has moved horizontal," Mrs. Samperi said.

"Ma," Jessamine said, breaking away from Milo with a gasp. "What are you doing here?"

"You mean here in my own home? It's a mystery, dear," Mrs. Samperi said. "Hello, Milo. Have you eaten?"

"He's not hungry, Ma," Jessamine said.

"He looks famished to me," Mrs. Samperi said.

Jessamine covered her face. "This is worse than high school."

"This never happened in high school. You were too standoffish," Mrs. Samperi mused. She made her way into the room and sat on the other side of Jessamine's bed. "So what happened? And I don't mean just now, unless you particularly want to talk about it. I mean earlier today. I got a call, scared me half to death. Your brothers are all here, too."

"Oh, goody," Jessamine said. She uncovered her face and turned to Milo. "You should escape now before she turns on you and you can't get away."

"There are snacks on the counter, Milo. Help yourself, but you'd better hurry before the boys eat everything. Don't be afraid to jump in there. Elbows out," Mrs. Samperi urged.

"Thank you, Mrs. Samperi," Milo replied.

"Call me Marie," Mrs. Samperi said.

"Thank you, Marie," he amended before grabbing his gun and shoes and heading out the door. Once he was safely in the hallway, he closed the door and leaned on it, trying to gather his senses. The morning had been a confusing jumble of too-big emotions. Milo needed to focus, to keep his mind on what was important. His job, no matter what, was to keep Jessamine safe.

By now he knew her well enough to realize that she would rebound from this morning's misadventure with anger and determination. In an effort to prove she couldn't be defeated or intimidated, she could very well get herself killed. Her stalker meant business. If he had gotten to her at the police station, he could get to her anywhere. Milo needed a plan, and he needed it fast. She would take a nap, and when she woke, he needed to be ready. He also needed backup, and he knew exactly where to find it.

CHAPTER 15

Conversation came to a standstill when Milo entered the kitchen. The four Samperi brothers were gathered around a massive tray overloaded with various kinds of salami, cheese, olives and crispy breadsticks Jessamine informed him were called *grissini*.

Moss was the first to approach, a grissini hanging out of his mouth like a walrus tusk. He squinted at Milo, focusing on the bottom part of his face. "That's some rash you have on your lips and chin, Milo. Looks painful."

"Eczema," Milo lied.

"I didn't get eczema like that until I was married," Giovanni chimed in. "How's Jess?"

"Subdued," Milo said, and now he had everyone's attention.

"That bad?" Joe asked.

"Yes, it was bad," Milo said. "I swear I only stepped away from her for a moment to use the bathroom."

"No one's blaming you," Joe said.

"I'm blaming myself. And then there's Jess who willingly left the room to take a call." He had told her not to feel guilty about it, but on further inspection, he was irritated. Her phone addiction could have gotten her killed. He picked up a plate, loaded it with goodies from the heaping platter, and took a seat at the massive kitchen island. After a few bites, he tossed down his breadstick in disgust. "The thing is, I'm in love with her."

"Yeah, we got that," Giovanni said. The brothers took the other chairs at the island and began to eat.

"I can't get an in with her," Milo said.

"Looks like you got in a little," Moss said, motioning to Milo's chapped lips.

"That's only because she's upset. Once she rebounds, she's not going to want to have anything to do with me again," Milo complained.

"Hey, look how well you know her after such a short amount of time," Benny said.

"She's so…" Milo balled his fists in frustration.

"We know," Joe agreed.

"Her walls are too high. How do I get past them?" Milo asked.

"You can't. There's too much competition," Moss informed him sadly.

"The judge?"

Moss chuckled. "Milo, my son, don't be daft. The competition isn't another dude. It's the job."

"The job," Milo agreed, letting his forehead thump on the table. He sat up and inspected the other men at the table. "You guys know her better than anyone. What do I need to do? What does she want in a man?"

"Someone strong," Joe said.

"But tender," Benny added.

"Smart," Giovanni chimed in.

"But with a sense of humor," Moss inserted.

Milo let his gaze travel around the island. "Basically you're saying she wants all of you rolled into one man."

"Hmm, I never thought of it like that," Moss said. "Good luck. Maybe you could become a priest. Lots of openings these days."

"No, what I need to do is get her away from work. Would that be okay?" Milo looked at Joe for approval.

"She hasn't had a day off in sixteen years. I think we could swing it," Joe said.

"Wait, without Jessamine there, who's going to boss us around and micromanage everything?" Moss asked.

"We could always ask Ma to stop by for a few days," Giovanni suggested.

"That's assuming he can do it. Jess has closer contact with her phone than that guy on *Star Trek* with the ring," Moss said.

"What are you talking about?" Giovanni asked. "What guy? What ring?"

"You know, the precious or whatever," Moss said.

"That's *The Lord of the Rings*. Stop trying to make literary references you in no way understand," Giovanni commanded.

"You got what I meant," Moss argued.

"Only because I know the warped way your half a brain works," Giovanni groused. "He's right, though. Jess isn't going to go without a fight. She fights dirty, and it's terrifying."

"I'm working on something that will keep her safe and get her away for a while," Milo said. "Obviously I can't do it alone. I'm going to need your support, and before you reply, I need you to know I'm not the same stupid kid I was in high school. And even though I don't have an actual job right now, I have prospects. I have references."

"We know, we've looked into them," Joe said, smiling in a way that was more chilling than friendly. "Believe us, Milo, if we didn't already trust you, you wouldn't be guarding our sister."

"Duly noted," Milo said.

Mrs. Samperi entered the room then. "She's sleeping. Why is there so much food left? Are you sick?"

"We were talking, Ma," Benny said.

"About what?" Mrs. Samperi asked.

"Milo's plan to kidnap Jess," Moss said.

"It had better be good. She's smart and good at escaping tight spaces," Mrs. Samperi said, helping herself to a plate of cheese and salami.

"She won't be able to contact you for a few days. Whoever this guy is has access to private information that keeps leading him right to her. I'm not taking any more chances. I won't tell you where we're going, and you won't be able to talk to her."

"For how long?" Joe asked.

"For as long as it takes to keep her safe and figure out what's going on," Milo replied.

"If this were a movie, you'd be the bad guy, the one we trusted who was right under our noses all along," Moss said.

"If I'm the bad guy, who's the person I tossed down the stairs this afternoon?" Milo mused.

"You really threw him down the stairs?" Mrs. Samperi asked.

"All the way down, but he must be made of plastic or something because he bounced back up and got away," Milo said, sounding glum. If only he had tackled the guy and waited for help to arrive. But he hadn't been able to keep a cool head with Jessamine in danger. He had *re*-acted instead of acted in a calm, controlled manner. Never again. If he ever got the chance to come face to face with her stalker again, the guy wouldn't get away; Milo would make sure of it.

"What did you do in the marines?" Moss asked.

"I'm not at liberty to say," Milo said. His work in military intelligence had been so far undercover it probably wouldn't be de-classified for another fifty years or so.

"That's so cool," Moss replied. "I should have been a soldier."

"They have IQ requirements," Giovanni informed him.

"Boys, manners," Mrs. Samperi snapped. "Sorry, Milo, sometimes they forget themselves."

"It's really all right, Marie. I understand large families." He glanced worriedly toward the stairs. How long would Jessamine sleep? Normally she only snoozed a few hours, far fewer than he did. But now she was exhausted, emotionally and physically drained. Would she sleep all night?

"Would it make you feel better to stay over, dear?" Mrs. Samperi offered.

"It would, yes," Milo answered.

"Good because I already made up the guest room," Mrs. Samperi said.

"Can you excuse me for a minute? I need to make a phone call to get some things arranged," Milo said.

"Take as long as you need," Mrs. Samperi replied.

Milo eased away from the table, phone in hand. Time wasn't all that he needed. Right now, an extra dose of courage would come in handy. When Jessamine learned the full truth about his life, how would she react? There was only one way to know for sure.

CHAPTER 16

*J*essamine slept longer than any other time in her life since she had the flu five years ago. When she woke, Milo was leaning in her doorway, one shoulder propped on the jamb.

"How long have you been there?" she asked.

"Twelve hours," he said, smiling.

She glanced at the clock. She had slept an unbelievable twelve hours. Her stomach rumbled. She hadn't eaten since breakfast the day before. Milo entered the room uninvited, perched on the edge of the bed, and placed his palms on the mattress on either side of her face, leaning. "We need to talk," he announced.

"Can I eat, shower, and brush my teeth first?" she asked.

"After," he said. "Don't worry, I'll keep it brief. We're going away."

"Where are we going?" she asked, not ready to dig her heels in until she had some answers.

"Someplace safe," he said.

"It's safe here," she said.

He shook his head. "It's not. If he found you at the police station, he could find you anywhere. He knows this is where you're staying."

She opened her mouth to protest, but he preempted her. "Do you want to put your parents at risk?"

She closed her mouth. "Where?"

"I can't tell you until we get there," he said. "No one can know where we're going, *no one.*"

"My family doesn't do well with not knowing things," she said.

"They've already agreed. It's all set. As soon as you're showered, dressed, and fed, we'll be on our way."

"I need to tie up some loose work threads," she said.

He shook his head again.

She sat up. "What do you mean no? You don't own me, you don't get to say where I go or when."

"Jessamine, I have spent an entire week following you around like one of those little dogs Hollywood types carry in their purses. I went from being a marine to being a show pony, and I haven't complained. In fact, I've kind of enjoyed standing around watching you work or watching you do anything, for that matter. You have called the shots on every decision that's been made this week. You've been in complete control, and I haven't made a peep. You're a strong woman who knows what she wants, good for you, that's fantastic. But things are different now. Your safety was compromised in a fundamental way, and this is the point where I take over. So get dressed because we're leaving in an hour."

"And if I refuse?" she asked.

"Don't test me, Jess," he said, his tone steely and stern. Softening, he continued, "Let's be friends. Trust that I'm doing this for your good." They stared each other down. She seemed to be looking for cracks, poking his façade for any weakness she could exploit. Suddenly all the staring contests he'd had as a kid were worth it because he didn't blink. Eventually she lay back down.

"Fine, now let's talk about last night. You know that was a blip," she said.

"I do know that, actually," he said. "Doesn't mean I didn't enjoy it."

"Some might argue you took advantage of me in my fragile emotional state," she said.

"Anyone who would call you fragile has clearly never met you and their judgment can't be trusted," he said.

One corner of her mouth turned up slightly. "I didn't think there was a right answer, but it turns out you found one."

"Just so we're clear, there will be no hanky-panky between us, no matter how much you beg," he said.

"Just so we're clear, my mom once told me the only thing a lady should ever chase is a runaway dog, and I don't own a dog," she said.

"Good, because I can't have my head crowded with other things. I need to focus on my job."

"So you've mentioned," she said, sounding irritated now. "Can you leave, or are you planning to stand outside the bathroom while I shower?"

"Outside?" he said. "For safety purposes, I really think I need to be in the room with you. And the safest option would be for you to leave the curtain open."

"Way to keep your focus," she said. "Go away, I want to get clean."

"I'll meet you downstairs. I'll be the guy sitting in the kitchen letting your mom stuff me with homemade donuts," he said.

"We call them *zeppole*," she said.

"I know, but I wanted to watch your mouth move when you said it," he replied, and then he leaned forward and brushed a feather soft kiss to her lips, so fast she didn't have time to respond, even if she'd wanted to.

"I thought you said no kissing," she reminded him.

"That was for luck, it doesn't count," he said.

"How often should I expect your rules to change?" she asked.

"As often as necessary," he said. "Look alive, soldier. You now have fifty minutes."

"Or what?" she asked.

"Or I'll carry you out of here as is," he said.

"You've gone mad with power," she said.

"I was due for a turn," he replied. "Get moving before I kiss you again. A man can only take so much temptation."

"I've seen me first thing in the morning, not so much temptation," she said.

"Then you should definitely see yourself through my eyes for a whole different perspective," he said. "Chop, chop."

She tossed a pillow at him, but it was too late, he was already out of the room. Jessamine blinked at the ceiling, trying to get her mind in order. She was in a muddle today, and that was so unlike her. For as long as she could remember, she had embraced each day with purpose, always having something on her agenda to do that day. Now she had only to get ready, and then Milo was in charge. Jessamine didn't like it. She hadn't spent a lifetime waging war for supremacy with four larger-than-life brothers, only to hand over control to some stranger.

In Milo's defense, he hadn't fought her on anything besides lunch all week. And after her mother started sending food for him, he hadn't bothered her about it again. He had surprised her with his willingness to stand aside and take direction. She had pictured every day as a potential argument, but he had capitulated to her control with almost disappointing ease. Not that she wanted him to argue, but a little show of spine and spirit would have been nice. And now there was too much spine and spirit in the mix.

I am such a complete mess, she thought. She wanted to be in control, she didn't want to be in control. What was her problem? And if she couldn't figure it out, how could anybody else? Lucky for her, she wasn't in the market for a partner. Her career had never been hotter. Now was not the time to add a man into the mix, and especially not Milo Eliopoulos. He was charming and handsome, a devastatingly good dancer and kisser, but that was where it ended. Jessamine had always pictured herself with someone whose ambition matched her own. Milo seemed so content to just…be. He was a veteran, and she respected that, but she needed someone driven, someone who could match her energy and passion. And then there was his wife.

He didn't act like she thought a widower should act. For someone who had only recently taken off his wedding ring, he had certainly recovered and moved on with remarkable speed. How could

Jessamine trust that his so-called feelings for her were real when he had been able to get over a wife of more than a decade in a heartbeat?

She needed to face the facts: as much as she liked Milo, as much as he made her laugh and she was comfortable in his presence (comfortable enough to ask for a kiss when one was needed), he wasn't for her. He wasn't deep enough, driven enough. He just wasn't *enough.* He would continue to be a pal, as he was now, but that was all she ever envisioned for them. And judging by the shallowness of his feelings, he would get over her soon, if he actually liked her as much as he said he did. Jessamine had her doubts. They barely knew each other. How could he have formed such an attachment to her already? Further proof of his shallowness, in her opinion. He was fun, but he wasn't for her.

When she reached for her phone, it wasn't there. Her mother had a habit of charging it for her, as she had a habit of doing everything Jessamine could do for herself. She trotted to the shower, tamping down her frustration. Even when she was a kid, she hadn't liked being treated like a kid. Her mother was a coddler, and she's been cursed with a daughter who couldn't stand to be coddled. The family liked to joke that Jessamine's first words had been, "I do it myself," and it was probably only a slight exaggeration. Some of her earliest memories were of trying to outdo her brothers, of wanting to be the best, the biggest, the most of everything. She'd had a wonderful childhood, but she hadn't enjoyed being a child. Independence, accomplishment, and responsibility had always been foremost in her mind. She had seemingly never wanted or needed to be taken care of by anyone.

Those character traits made her current situation all the more stifling. Her hard-won independence had been wiped away by forces outside her control. First she had to move in with her parents, and now she had to abandon everything familiar and follow Milo to an unknown location, now when she was the busiest she had ever been. It was so frustrating she wanted to scream.

Downstairs she found Milo in the kitchen with her mother, laughing and chatting like old friends. Of course her mother would like Milo. He had a big appetite and a good sense of humor. They turned smiling at her approach.

"Right on time," Milo commented.

"Mom, have you seen my phone?" Jessamine asked, ignoring him. She wasn't ready because he had told her to get ready; she was ready because it was time to get up and get ready.

"Would you like some breakfast, dear? I made the eggs you like," Mrs. Samperi said, turning to reach for a plate.

"Eggs are fine, Ma, thanks. About my phone," Jessamine began.

"Coffee's ready, too," Mrs. Samperi said.

It was never a good sign when her mother hedged. Normally a straight shooter, if she wasn't saying something flat out, it meant trouble. "Ma, did you accidentally break my phone or something?"

"I took your phone," Milo said.

Jessamine turned in a slow circle to face him. "What?"

"I think I'll nip into the laundry room, make sure you didn't leave anything behind," Mrs. Samperi said, beating a hasty retreat to the far side of the kitchen.

"Can I have it, please?" Jessamine demanded, her palm extended in his direction.

"You know what's interesting? Your mom's not afraid of any of your brothers, but she's afraid of you. I wonder why that is," Milo mused.

"Experience and common sense. My phone, please," she reiterated.

"It's not here," Milo said.

"It's not here?" she repeated.

"I gave it to the FBI," he said.

"You did what?"

"They're taking it apart, checking for traces, for bugs, trying to figure out if that's how he's tracking you," Milo said.

"When will it be finished?" she asked.

He shrugged.

"I'm curious to know why you thought you could take my phone and give it to the FBI while I was sleeping and without my permission," she said.

"Experience and common sense?" he tried.

"Are you trying to be cute?" she said.

"I don't actually have to try. I was born this way," he said.

"Remember when I hit you in the face? I'm angrier now than I was then," she warned him.

"Are you trying to tell me now would be a good time to kiss you? Because that's what I'm taking from this conversation."

"Milo, you had no right to take my phone, and I want it back. Now."

"You can't take your phone where we're going, and I didn't know how else to get it from you. The FBI needs to sweep it, and you've been putting them off too long."

"I can't be without my phone. My entire life is on that phone," she said.

"Think of it like a vacation. People don't take their work phones on vacation," he said.

"I do, or I would, if I'd ever taken a vacation," she said.

"You're angry now, but I think in time you're going to thank me for this." She was giving him the death stare. He resisted the urge to take a step back, mostly because he was already sitting. "Or maybe not. Either way it's a moot point because your phone is probably in a few pieces by now."

"Fine, then I'm not going," she said.

"Oh, you're going," he said.

"No. I have too much work to do, and Moss's wedding is coming up. His head's only half in the game, and soon he'll be going on his honeymoon. It's a bad time to take off."

"It's a perfect time to take off, and it's all arranged. I can call your brothers, if you like, have them tell you in person to go away," he suggested.

He had gotten to her parents, infected her brothers, was in cahoots with the local police and FBI. Was no one on Jessamine's side?

"The producers..." she tried.

"Would rather you stay alive than alter their shooting schedule.

Plus they said they've already got a ton of good footage. They're going to play with the timeline, make it work," Milo said.

"What if my brothers have questions while they're on site?" she said. She was usually there every single day, in constant communication. Sometimes her designs were fluid. How would it work if she wasn't there to oversee them?

"I'll be their go-between. If they have questions, they'll ask me, and I'll relay them to you," he said. "It's going to be fine, Jess. You might even learn to relax and have fun."

"I am relaxed, and I have plenty of fun," she snapped, her arms crossed, her body tense.

"Hmm," he said, taking in her rigid stance with a head to toe sweeping glance. "Maybe you'll learn to have a different kind of fun."

"Is that what this is about? Some clever ploy to take me to a deserted island and make me fall in love with you? Because I have news, it's not happening. You could take away all my freedoms and lock me in a padded cell with only you to stare at all day, and I still guarantee I will not fall for you. You might as well forget it," she said.

"I wasn't insinuating anything, but the fact that you think I was makes me wonder what's on your mind. Are you having trouble thinking of anything but me? Is that why you're so irritable?" he asked.

"Reasons I'm irritable, chapter one: I haven't eaten in twenty four hours. You're kidnapping me, and you stole my phone," she said.

He put his hands on her shoulders and steered her to a chair. "No wonder you're cranky; you need sustenance. Sit and let Milo take care of you, *kardia mou*." He made her a plate of eggs and a mug of coffee. While she worked on eating the eggs, he made toast.

"My brothers used to do that," she said.

"What?" he asked.

"Speak Italian to get girls to like them."

"That wasn't Italian, that was Greek. Did it work for your brothers?"

"They're all married or engaged, so presumably," she said.

"You never used it on some guy?" he asked.

"Yes, but I only ever say it in anger, so it doesn't have the same effect," she said.

"I only know the good words," he assured her.

She watched him a while longer before speaking again. "My mom doesn't let anyone work in her kitchen but her, and yet somehow you've taken over. How have you brainwashed everyone in my family?" she asked between bites of egg and sips of coffee.

"I have a way with women. Well, most women," he said eyeing her while he buttered her toast.

"My brothers like you, too," she pointed out. She'd brought home the occasional boyfriend over the years. Her brothers had disliked them all. But Milo Eliopoulos—unemployed widowed veteran and former bad boy of their school—was A-okay in their combined opinion. Jessamine didn't get it. Were they seeing something she wasn't, or had she reached that point of spinsterhood where her family was desperate to unload her on the nearest willing taker?

"Maybe they understand that I have your best interest at heart, despite whatever you might think," he said. "Better?" he indicated her empty plate.

"Thank you."

"Are you ready to go?"

"No," she said.

"Are you actually ready to go and you're saying no out of stubbornness?" he guessed.

"Yes," she said. "Ma, you can come out now. We're leaving."

Mrs. Samperi poked her head from around the corner. "I suppose I should pretend I wasn't listening, but I'm not that good an actress." She hugged Jessamine. "Take care, dear. Be safe. Don't do anything crazy. We love you."

"Thanks, Ma. I love you, too." Jessamine returned her tight hug while Milo fetched her luggage and loaded it in his car. She had left her parents' home at eighteen without a twinge or backwards glance. But now, when she was only going for a few days, she wanted to stay, to cling to everything that was familiar. Her mother must have sensed as much.

"It's going to be okay, Jess. If we didn't believe that, we'd never let him take you," Mrs. Samperi said.

"Why do you trust him so much?" Jessamine whispered.

Mrs. Samperi let her go and smoothed the hair off her face. "Sometimes it takes the people who love you to see what you can't."

"No idea what that means, Ma," Jessamine said.

"Good thing for you you'll have plenty of time to figure it out," Mrs. Samperi replied and, with one final kiss to her forehead, waved her only daughter away.

CHAPTER 17

"Where are we going?" Jessamine asked as soon as they were enclosed in Milo's car.

"I can't tell you yet. And before you let loose with whatever is on your pretty lips, let me tell you that I don't trust that my car isn't bugged," he said.

"You really think he'd go that far?" Jessamine asked, her tone loaded with skepticism.

"Without knowing who he is, I have no idea how far he'd go," Milo said. "I swept the car for tracking devices, but they're bigger and easier to find. Microphones can be an invisible dot, no bigger than a freckle."

"You've watched too many spy movies," she told him.

He gave her a secret little smile she couldn't interpret and faced forward again.

"Is it far?" she asked.

He shook his head, refusing to answer out loud. Jessamine thought he was being paranoid, but it wasn't as if she could make him talk to her. Without her phone as a distraction, she had only her sketchbook of ideas. Right now it was too bumpy to write or draw, and she wasn't in the mood. Her face turned to stare out the window, watching as the terrain eased from that of their small town to the neighboring rolling hills of horse country. Kentucky was a beautiful place. The aforementioned green hills, combined with miles of wooden or stone fences made her feel a bit like she was in Ireland. She heard once that was why so many people from the United Kingdom settled in the state, because it reminded them of home.

Eventually the rolling hills gave way to pine trees and woods. Milo turned into what Jessamine originally thought was a dirt road. When she realized it was a dirt lane, she sat up and took interest. The long lane wove back and forth between a grove of trees and ended abruptly in front of a rundown little ranch house. A woman opened the front door and stood on the porch to greet them.

"Will she be staying with us?" Jessamine asked.

"No."

"Was she here to clean or something?" Jessamine asked.

Milo chuckled. "No. That's my sister."

"Oh, oops. I didn't know you had a sister," she said.

He grinned at her. "I have five."

"You have five sisters?" she exclaimed. "How did I never know this?"

"I was the baby of the family, and they're all a lot older," Milo explained.

"Is this her house?" Jessamine asked, glad she hadn't made comment on the home's dilapidated state.

"No," Milo said. He exited the car without further comment and ascended the porch. Jessamine trailed slowly behind. The woman's eyes were on her. What had Milo told his family about her? And why had it never occurred to her before that he had family? He had mentioned his mother, but Jessamine hadn't asked any follow up questions. They had spent all day every day together the past week, and she hadn't asked him one question about his life. How shallow and self-involved could she be?

"You must be Jessamine. I'm Amara," the woman said, holding out her hand. Jessamine shook it, feeling uncharacteristically shy.

"How do you do? It's nice to meet you," she replied, shaking

Amara's hand in return. It wasn't until she was on the porch that she saw the little girl's face poking through the curtain, spying on them. Neither Amara nor Milo mentioned her, so Jessamine followed suit and pretended she wasn't there.

"Milo's told us so many things about you, and of course I've seen you on TV," Amara continued. "Is that okay to say? I'm not some kind of stalker fan or anything. But, being local, everyone is sort of following what's going on with you and your family."

"No, please, it's nice to hear that. I hope we're representing the hometown all right, even with all the yelling," Jessamine said.

"Pfft, if people don't understand the yelling, they've clearly never been part of a big family," Amara said.

"I know, right?" Jessamine agreed, smiling. "If your family doesn't have at least four children, then no comments on our volume."

"Being Mediterranean helps too, I think," Amara added. "I bet big families in Scandinavia and Britain all whisper politely. They probably don't even use their hands when they talk." For emphasis, she waved her arms expressively.

Jessamine laughed. "And do you think they use food to represent love? Not hardly."

"I'm going to like you," Amara said, smiling in return. To Milo she added, "Everything is all set here. Do you need anything before I go?"

"I think we're good," Milo replied. They hugged and Amara turned to Jessamine.

"It was so nice to meet you, Jessamine. You live up to the hype."

"Thank you," Jessamine said. "I'll be sure to let the producers know they're on target."

"Not the show's hype, Milo's hype." She squeezed his arm and flitted down the stairs before going to her car and starting it. They watched her until she was out of sight, and that was when Jessamine remembered the little girl.

"She forgot her daughter," Jessamine said.

"No, she didn't," Milo said.

"But the little girl..." she pointed to the house. "Please don't tell me there is no little girl and the house is haunted."

"The house is not haunted, and the little girl is mine. Surprise." He sounded nervous and uncertain.

"You have a daughter?" Jessamine said slowly.

"Yes. She's twelve, and I'm sure she'd like to meet you. Is that okay?"

"Absolutely," Jessamine replied, though she wasn't sure she meant it. She had never once figured a kid into the equation. She wasn't great with kids, not having a lot of experience with anyone outside her younger brothers. And they weren't that far behind her in age.

"She's a little shy," Milo explained. "It's been a tough year."

"Okay," Jessamine said. She had no idea what else to say. Waves of shock poured over her. He had been married for more than a decade. Why should it come as a surprise that he had a child? Because he'd never mentioned her? Did he have more than one? Was an entire brood inside? Did he expect her to take care of them? She tugged his sleeve, holding him back. "There's only one, right?"

"Just the one," he said.

Jessamine wasn't sure if he sensed her nervousness or he was trying to cover his own anxiety. Whatever the reason, he clasped her hand as he opened the door and led her inside. "Iz, this is the woman I was telling you about who is going to be staying here for a bit," he said after they were safely inside.

The house was dim. It took Jessamine's eyes a few minutes to adjust from the brightness outside. When she could see again, she relaxed and offered up a smile. Before her stood a shy and unassuming little girl, her hair a greasy curtain that covered an almost invisible face. "Hello. Iz?"

"Hi. It's short for Isadora."

"Isadora, that's beautiful," Jessamine said.

"My mom picked it for a famous dancer, Isadora Duncan," Iz replied, a tiny bit of pride intruding into her tone.

"I've heard of her," Jessamine said. "She was really spectacular. Was your mom a dancer?"

Iz nodded.

"Did she teach your dad to dance?" Jessamine guessed.

Iz nodded again, smiling a little.

"Do you dance, too?"

Iz shook her head, her expression dimming.

"I didn't know how to dance when I was your age, either, but I got better at it," Jessamine told her.

"Are you a dancer?" Iz asked, her frown deepening.

"Not professionally, I do it for fun. I'm a designer, I design and decorate houses."

Iz nodded again. She was so expressive. Jessamine could see her digesting the information, trying to figure out exactly what it meant.

"Let's show Jess the house, Iz," Milo commented. "This is the living room and kitchen." He led her down the hall. "Here's the master bedroom. Next door is the bathroom, and here's the room you'll be sharing with Iz. Laundry is in the basement."

It was hard for Jessamine to see the house as it was because she was so used to seeing things as they could be. If he knocked out the entire back wall of the house, he could make a new kitchen and laundry area, add a new master suite, and add an additional bedroom with a jack-and-jill bathroom. Or would it be best to add a second floor over half the house? No, it was better suited as a ranch. Knocking out the back was the way to go. Belatedly, she realized he was waiting for her to comment on the house. Now that she made herself focus on it in its current state, it became even harder to find something nice to say. "It's pleasant," she said. "Cozy." Standing at the edge of Isadora's room, she wasn't sure which thought was most alarming—that the room was stark white with no decoration or personalization or that she would soon be sharing the space with a twelve year old. Her mind clicked through all the ways the room could be improved, starting with the color. Girls that age usually had a thing for turquoise. Jessamine had done four turquoise tween rooms in the last year alone. If they knocked out the back wall, there would be plenty of space for a new walk-in closet and reading nook.

"Sorry," she said, snapping to attention again. "My mind tends to wander when I look at houses. Occupational hazard. What's your favorite color, Iz?"

Iz jumped with surprise at having a direct question aimed at her. "Ivory."

Jessamine beamed at her. "Really? Ivory's so interesting. Do you prefer gold or silver?"

"Gold," Iz whispered uncertainly.

"Awesome," Jessamine replied, her eyes still on the room. Everything snapped into focus at once, the layers of gold and ivory, a few easy-care plants for color, and a hint of light pink to keep it fun and feminine. She hadn't done an ivory room in forever, and this one... well, this one wasn't her job. She couldn't go to the store and buy anything. She couldn't even order online because Milo had made her swear not to use her credit card in order to remain untraceable. She was stuck in this ugly space for the foreseeable future with no way to change it or make it better. But poor Isadora was stuck in the ugly space for life.

It was Thursday, Jessamine realized. Shouldn't Iz be in school? "Are you homeschooled?" *Please don't say yes,* she silently pled. Did she have to spend all day with the girl, too?

"I let her stay home today because you were coming. It's the most excitement we've had in a while," Milo said. "Iz, why don't you work on your homework?"

"All I have left is math, Dad, and I need your help."

"Uh," Milo said, his eyes darting to Jessamine.

"Go ahead, please. I'll bring in my suitcase and get settled."

Arranging her things didn't take as long as Jessamine hoped it might. Since there was nowhere to unpack, she merely dragged her suitcase to an unoccupied corner and set it upright. She sat on her bed and stared around the small space. Iz's bed was a mere two feet away.

Being the only girl meant Jessamine had never shared a room before. She hadn't gone to college so there had been no roommate to reckon with. When she was little and before her family moved to the big house, she'd shared a bathroom with her brothers, but she hardly remembered. Now she would be sharing with both Iz and Milo.

No matter where she had lived, she'd always tried to make her space beautiful, but as she looked around the dumpy little space, she thought maybe she had met her match. She couldn't decorate this space, both because it wasn't hers and because she had no access to anything she normally used. She couldn't go to her favorite stores and buy paint, lights, furniture, and accessories. She couldn't even order online because she couldn't use her credit card.

Her thumbs itched to text someone, anyone, and distract herself from her plight. What was going on with her brothers? How were they doing on the jobsite without her? She felt caged, and that made her irritable. How had she wound up in this situation—trapped in a stranger's home with no way to communicate with the outside world and nothing to do? Her leg bounced, antsy with unused energy. *It's only a few days; you can survive anything for a few days.* Could she, though? She missed her house, her car, her job, her phone. Mostly, she missed her independence. She had spent her whole life trying to control everything—her environment, her work, even her brothers. How had it all been taken away in one fell swoop?

Her gaze drifted to the window. It was a cheap aluminum frame. She could easily pop it out and run for freedom. And then what? Where could she go from here? She couldn't go back home, and she wouldn't put her family in danger. She couldn't run off somewhere and stay in a hotel because she had no idea how her stalker was tracking her. And lately everywhere she went, she was recognized. She was stuck, stuck, stuck in Milo's tiny dump and had never felt more claustrophobic. Now she had to go back to the living room with Milo. And his *daughter.*

CHAPTER 18

Over the last couple of weeks, Milo had gotten to know Jessamine pretty well. He'd had nothing else to do but stand by and make a study of her. He knew, therefore, exactly what was going on when she escaped to the bedroom and stayed. She hated the house. How could she not? He did, too. It was ugly, cheap, dumpy, and depressing. She hadn't expected Iz. He probably should have warned her, but he hadn't been able to find the words. He had no words for anything. For the last year and a half, his world had been in complete upheaval. He had lost his wife, quit his job, moved halfway across the country, and resumed life as a fulltime father. He and Iz were only beginning to take their first steps toward normalcy. How was he supposed to explain everything to Jessamine when he was still finding his way himself?

Bringing her to his house had seemed like the perfect answer to keep her safe, but maybe it was born of his desperation to get close to her. He couldn't say for certain, and that bothered him. He was supposed to be putting the job first. But his reaction to her, his feelings for her, his desire to be with her, were so strong they clouded his judgment. All he knew was that in the real world, where she was firmly in control of everything, she had no time for him. The walls she'd made were like everything else she built—solid and immovable. He had needed to do something drastic. And his home was safe. Working in intelligence for so many years had taught him a few things about hiding paper trails. No one could find his house through any of the usual channels. He had hidden his ownership in so many layers it would take years to uncover. It was private, and he had taken measures to alert himself to anyone's arrival or presence on the property. It may not look like much, but it was safe.

That thought brought him reassurance. Whatever his motives, Jessamine was safe at his house. If he thought she wasn't, he would never allow her to be near Iz and put her in danger. Iz was a bit of a loose thread, of course. Milo had warned her repeatedly not to tell anyone at school Jessamine was staying with her. He had been frank, warning her of the danger Jessamine was in. Her reply had broken his heart.

Don't worry, Dad. I don't talk to anyone anyway. It's the upside of having no friends. Milo had no reply for that. He'd always had a big group of friends. True, they'd been losers and rebels like him, but they had been his friends nonetheless. He had no idea how to deal with his shy, insecure child. Every time he tried to make a suggestion of how to help her, she gave him a look that was almost pitying, as if he couldn't begin to understand her world. And she was correct. He had no idea what it was like to be a girl and only a dim memory of what it was to be twelve. She'd been through so much. He had no idea how to help her. He also had the vague sense he was failing miserably. His only hope was that she would realize how much he loved her, that someday she would understand how much he had given up to be there for her. His once promising career was now dead. He had nothing but her and an undying love for a woman who barely knew he existed. If he thought about his life too closely, he could get really depressed really fast. Thankfully Milo had never been the type to dwell. He tended to live in the world of possibilities, of what might be, if he only kept striving.

After he explained Iz's math homework, he went to find Jessamine. She was sitting on the bed, staring at the wall in silence, looking like a red rose miraculously growing out of a trash heap. He had grown used to the dumpy atmosphere of his house; seeing her there made him realize afresh how bad it was.

"If you're looking for a way to tunnel out, you should know I'm monitoring the sewers," he said.

She looked up at him with a smile that didn't reach her eyes. He held out his hand to her. "Come with me, I want to show you something." She put her hand in his and allowed him to lead her from the room and outside. It was a measure of how off kilter she felt that she did so without protest. Jessamine Samperi was a woman who was not easily led anywhere. They walked through the dingy house and outside a few paces to a small barn surrounded by rolling pastures. They both took a breath, as if shaking off the oppressive atmosphere of the house. Jessamine blinked and looked around as if just waking up.

"This is pretty," she exclaimed. The barn was as aesthetically pleasing as the house wasn't, and the green pasture behind it looked as if it had been painted there by a talented artist.

Milo leaned on the fence and stared out at the rolling countryside. "When I was a kid, we lived next to a farm that had a horse. The horse and I were good friends. He used to come to the fence whenever I was outside, hang his head over, and let me pet him. I thought there was nothing better than owning horses. To a poor kid, the sixth in an already too crowded family, it seemed like the most obvious sign of wealth and arrival in the world. I vowed someday I would have a horse, that my kids would grow up with them. And then I joined the marines and spent the majority of a decade overseas. When I left the military and moved back home, I looked for a place to have horses. This place spoke to me, the land, not the house," he finished with a wry glance at the dumpy house.

"It's really beautiful," Jessamine said, resting her hand on his bicep. The touch felt like an apology. He knew she felt bad about hating the house. She wasn't a mean person, not cruel enough to kick him when he was down. But she also couldn't help the way she felt. The house was atrocious. Her reaction to it was predictable.

"The great irony is that, now that I have the land, I still can't afford a horse," he added, his tone self-deprecating.

"Why didn't you tell me you had a daughter?" she asked.

"It never came up," he said.

"Milo," she said, giving his arm a painful squeeze. The woman was strong. He had to resist the urge to shake her off.

He sighed. "Because it was one more strike against me. I mean, if an unemployed, poverty-stricken widower had no chance with you, how was adding the fact that I'm a single father going to help?"

"Did you ever consider that my reasons for avoiding romance have nothing to do with you and everything to do with me? I'm too busy, too independent," she said.

"So you say, but if the right man came along and swept you off your feet, I think you'd change your tune," he said.

"You sound exactly like my mother. And my grandmother. And it's super annoying."

He put his arm around her shoulders and rubbed gently, easing the tension out of her right blade. She rested her head on his shoulder and let out a long-held breath. It was progress because usually he couldn't catch her long enough to touch her. The woman was always on the move, always doing something, always going somewhere, always texting on her phone. Now there was nowhere to go, nothing to do. Maybe he was on to something after all.

"I don't think I'm going to survive this," Jessamine murmured.

"Don't talk like that. He's not going to get near you again."

"Not that," she said impatiently, "I'm talking about *this*. Boredom and inactivity. I really think it might kill me or drive me out of my mind. I'm so jittery I feel like I'm going to explode."

"I felt the same way after I quit my job. Eventually you adjust and find a new rhythm," he said.

"I don't want to find a new rhythm. I like the old one," she snapped.

"It's temporary. Come on, Samperi, where's that toughness you're always bragging about? Are you really telling me you can't handle a few days of downtime?" He gave her shoulder a squeeze.

"I don't know. It's never happened before," she said.

He put his other arm around her and gave her a proper hug. "I know this is hard, but it's going to be okay, I promise you."

"You're being so nice, and I'm being such a whiny baby," she said.

"I keep telling you I am nice," he reminded her. "Why don't you believe me?"

She pulled back slightly so they were face to face. "We danced together at my freshman homecoming. I was fourteen, and you were a senior."

"We did?" he said, smiling. "I don't remember."

"I do," she said, her tone bitter.

"Did I push you down, hit you, trip you?" he asked.

She shook her head. "You were delightful. You taught me to dance. You were your most charming. I practically swooned with delight."

"Then why the tone?" he asked.

"After the dance, I sneaked outside to see you again. You were there with your friends, and you were making fun of me. You called me a dog. You made fun of my nose."

His jaw dropped. "I did?"

She nodded.

"I'm so, so sorry. But, Jess, you have to understand how completely idiotic I was at that age. I mean, I was almost terminally stupid. Do you know I got arrested three times for bashing the same mailbox? I was too stupid to find a new mailbox, I just kept going back to the same one. The third time I was arrested, the judge gave me the option of going to jail or going to the armed forces. *And I had to think about it.* He was so exasperated that he took the decision out of my hands. I can still hear his voice saying, 'Boy, you are all kinds of stupid. You're going to the marines, maybe they'll straighten you out.'"

She smiled a little. He gave her shoulders a gentle shake.

"I didn't mean it, you know," he added.

"How can you say that when you don't even remember?" she asked.

"Because, in addition to being an idiot, I was incredibly shallow. I never would have danced with you if I hadn't thought you were cute. Other girls asked me that night, and I said no. I only said those things to save face with my friends and get them off my back. Will you pretty please forgive me for being such a complete and total moron sixteen years ago? No pressure, but the mailbox I beat up already forgave me."

"I forgive you," she said.

He leaned forward and placed a few nibbling kisses on her jawline.

"You're kissing me," she informed him.

"It doesn't count if it's not on the lips," he said.

"Your rules are arbitrary and senseless," she informed him.

"Some might argue life is arbitrary and senseless, so we should grab onto it," he said.

"You're spouting gibberish in the hopes of distracting me into accepting another kiss," she guessed.

"An hour at my house, and look how well you know me," he said, but he stepped back and let her go. "Are you hungry?"

"Decidedly so, yes," she said.

"Good, I'll show you where the kitchen is so you can whip something up for us," he said.

She stopped short. "What?"

"I'm joking. We don't make prisoners cook for us until day two," he said.

"I don't actually know how to cook," Jessamine said. "My mom doesn't let anyone in the kitchen and, honestly, I've never had the time or inclination to learn."

"I've had a lot of time and a lot of inclination," Milo told her. He held the door for her as they returned to the dingy, cramped kitchen. She perched on a chair while he flitted around the tiny kitchen, chopping, stirring, frying.

"It smells really good," she commented, and he tossed her a smile. Outside it started to rain, and it wasn't long before the ceiling started to drip. Milo seemingly thought nothing of it. Jessamine watched, dismayed, as he absently reached for containers to set beneath the drips.

"Does it always do that?" she asked.

"What?" he asked, glancing up at her in confusion.

She motioned to the drips.

"Only when it rains," he said, resuming his work.

Jessamine made an impatient cluck of disapproval and he tossed her another smile. "I'm guessing you've never lived with a leaky ceiling," he said.

"It's beyond my ability to fathom living with such a thing," she said.

"Think of it like visiting an exotic new land, one with bad lighting and ceiling leakage."

"But the soffits and drywall and…"

He leaned over the counter to stuff a crouton on her mouth. "Shh, there, there."

"This isn't finished," she said, reaching for another crouton.

"Okay," he said in the easygoing way that should have annoyed her but instead made her relax and reach for the entire bag of croutons.

$\mathcal{M}$ilo didn't like to leave Jessamine, but he had to take his daughter to school. The last time he left her alone, she was attacked. This time she was safe at his house, but it still felt wrong, especially when he returned home and she was nowhere to be found. His panic meter jumped until he heard a sound on the roof.

Going back out again, he shaded his eyes against the morning sun and stared on top of his house. "Santa?" he called.

Jessamine poked her head over the edge, nearly giving him a heart attack for different reasons. "Oh, hey. Guess what I found in the barn."

"Roofing supplies," he guessed.

"Enough to do the whole roof. Why were they in there?" she asked

"As part of the seller's agreement, they agreed to provide a new roof. Apparently we have differing ideas on that because they supplied the materials but not the actual labor."

"I think I know why it's leaking," Jessamine called. "There's a problem with some of the flashing, it wasn't installed correctly. Come up here, I'll show you."

He grasped the ladder with both hands, put one foot up, and closed his eyes against a wave of nausea.

Jessamine's head poked over the side again. "What are you doing?"

"Am I up there yet?" Milo asked.

"You haven't actually taken a step," she told him.

He opened his eyes and moved away from the ladder. "Now seems like a good time to tell you I don't do heights."

"You're joking," she said.

"I could throw up to convince you, if you'd like," he said. "It's why I haven't attempted the roof myself. Also because I don't know how to do that."

"Does it bother you seeing me up here?" Jessamine asked.

"A little. I'm lying, a lot. Could you come down, please?"

"Would it make it worse if I did this?" She stood on one leg in a ballet pose, letting the rest of her body drape perilously over the edge. Milo was torn between wanting to cover his eyes and wanting to catch her in the likely event she fell. Covering his eyes won.

"Please, stop. I can't deal with that sort of thing."

"You know I've been climbing on roofs pretty much all my life. Balance and I are good friends," she said.

"Don't care, can't watch. Come down," he said, both of his hands pressed firmly over his eyes.

She shimmied down the ladder and peeled his hands off his eyes. "I'm back on terra firma," she said. "Hey, you actually do look pale and clammy. Are you all right?"

"I *really* don't like heights. Please don't go up again," he said.

"How can I put a new roof on if I don't go up the ladder?" she asked.

"You can't fix my roof," he said.

"I really can, it'll be a cinch. There's only one layer up there. Except for a couple of soft spots where the flashing needs replaced, I'm not going to have to tear off the old roof."

"I have no idea what you're talking about, but you can't fix my roof. You're a guest in my house, and I already owe you a thousand dollars."

"If I don't find something to do, some kind of outlet for my energy, I'm going to go insane. Have you seen *The Shining*? No work and no hobbies make Jessamine a dull girl. So if you don't want me to fix your roof, you'd better come up with a better project. Also, I'm fixing your roof and you can't stop me. And I already told you I don't care about the thousand dollars. You saved me from a guy with a knife. I think we're even."

"You could fall," he said.

"I could, but I probably won't, and even if I did, it's not that far," she said, eyeing the low roofline.

"You're talking about falling off the roof like it's jumping off the bottom step," Milo said. "It's high."

"Milo, do you understand that I've walked on five story beams without a harness?" Jessamine said. "This is sort of what I do. This is a cake job for me, in the scheme of things. The hardest part is going to be hauling the supplies up, and I found a lever and pulley in the barn, so I'm golden."

"Lever and pulley? What are you, MacGyver?"

"You're getting all worked up, and it's really okay. Watch, you'll see." Before he could protest again, she shimmied back up the ladder and picked up her hammer. "I'm going to repair this flashing and then we'll be set. The whole project shouldn't take more than three days." She peered over the edge at Milo. He was looking up at her. He opened his mouth to speak, but no sound came out. Instead his eyes crossed, his knees buckled, and he folded to the ground in an untidy heap.

Jessamine slid back down the ladder again and knelt over him, taking his limp fingers in hers. She touched his cheek, and his eyes fluttered.

"Did you seriously just faint?" she asked.

"No sympathy?" he asked, his voice weak.

"You weren't even the one up there. You passed out from *watching* me."

"Thanks for the recap," he said, closing his eyes and breathing deeply through his nose.

"Can you make it to the house?" she asked.

"My mind says yes, but my gut says bring me a bucket and leave me to the vultures," Milo said.

"Come on, sugar pants, upsy daisy," Jessamine said. She slid her arm beneath him and heaved, pulling him upright beside her. After an unsteady step, he leaned heavily on her as they slowly made their way to the house. "How were you a marine? I assume heights were involved in there sometime."

"They were, and I did it because I had to. Maybe if a drill sergeant were yelling at me while you're on the roof, I'd be able to handle it here, too," he said.

"Too bad we can't involve my mother. Sometimes the only difference between her and a drill sergeant is the garlic," Jessamine said. She deposited Milo on the couch and retrieved a glass of water and a cool cloth for his forehead.

"Thank you," he said. His voice sounded a little stronger. He took a sip of the water and set it aside. Jessamine pressed the cloth to his head.

"Better?" she asked. She was perched beside him on the edge of the couch, very close to his face. He reached for her, pulling her within touching range as his lips pressed to her neck.

"You're kissing me again," she noted.

"Doesn't count if they're half-delirious recovery kisses," he said. "You're aiding in my healing. This is what good nurses do."

"I think you've made a miraculous comeback. Are you going to be all right lying here while I get back to work?" she asked.

"What? You're going back up there after I swooned and everything?" he asked.

"I don't stop until the job is done. This is why you don't actually want a romance with me. I keep trying to warn you." She brushed her hand over his hair a few times. It was too short to rest on his forehead, but the washcloth had caused it to curl appealingly.

"You don't have to warn me. I already know who you are, and I want you anyway," he said.

"Men always want what they can't have. It's your nature."

He blew out a breath. "You are…"

"Difficult?" she guessed. "Standoffish? Guarded? Work obsessed?

Determined? Bossy? Stubborn? Cold? Untouchable? Frozen? Controlling? I've heard them all before."

"Lovely," he finished, his hand brushing her cheek. "Kind, generous, warm-hearted, funny."

"You are good, you are very, very good," she whispered, her fingers still sifting his hair.

"And I'm only half trying," he said, a blatant lie since he was giving it his all and then some.

She kissed his forehead and stood. "Lie still. One swoon a day is enough."

"How will I know if you fall off and die?" he asked.

"I'll scream. Otherwise, assume I'm fine," she said. She gave his cheek a little pinch and walked out the door. A minute later, he heard pounding on the roof. He closed his eyes against the vision of her pitching over the roof and lying broken on the ground. She was fine, she was a professional, she had done this a million times. Just because it was unfathomable to him didn't mean it was out of the ordinary for her. Meanwhile he turned her words over in his head. Did she really believe she was some untouchable ice princess? She was one of the warmest, most passionate women he knew. Did she believe she was too much for him? She was, but not the way she meant. She was out of his league, a thousand times, too pretty, too accomplished, too put together, even too famous. But in her mind, did she see it differently? Did she genuinely believe she was too much for him to handle, a liability? How was that possible? And if she believed that, how did he make her see the truth?

Lying on the couch feeling queasy while she re-roofed his house was probably not a good start. Or maybe it was. Maybe what Jessamine needed most was the freedom to be Jessamine without anyone trying to change or control her. Maybe what she wanted was to be loved for who she was exactly where she was. In the end, wasn't that what everyone wanted? It was what Milo wanted, to be loved despite his past, despite the baggage he still carried, despite his lack of job or any prospects. Despite the fact that, in the world's eyes, he was an abject failure. How could he expect Jessamine to believe he wanted her as she was if he wasn't willing to believe she could love him as he was?

When did I turn into a fifteen-year-old girl? Instead of lying on the couch pondering the meaning of true love, he got up and made lunch, hoping he wouldn't have to carry it out to her and see her on the roof again. But of course he did because, as she said, she didn't stop until the job was done.

Milo loaded a tray and walked straight out of the house, keeping his back to the roof.

"Come down for lunch," he called, staring at nothing as he spoke to her.

"I'm kind of busy. Can you bring it up?" she called.

"Hilarious. Come down or I'm going to start throwing stuff at you. I may faint like a nineteenth century Victorian housewife, but I throw like a twenty first century marine."

She shimmied down. When she was finally on solid ground, he was able to look at her again. "You're filthy." Whatever she had been working with had left her blackened from nose to toe.

"This charm offensive you have going on is wearing me down for sure," she said.

"I didn't say I didn't like it. It's adorable, you're like my own little chimney sweep. How's it going up on Death Mountain?"

"Quickly, almost too quickly," she said, sounding a bit morose.

It was on the tip of his tongue to suggest that she try to enjoy doing nothing for a change, but that wasn't loving her as she was. She liked to be busy; she liked to be working. "I could give you a list of other stuff that needs done, if you like."

"Really?" she asked, sitting up on her knees in excitement.

"As you may have guessed, I'm sort of hopeless at house stuff, minus cooking and cleaning, and it's about one squeaky floorboard from being declared an actual hovel."

"I would love to help, but I didn't want to intrude and overstep my bounds or offend you," she said.

"Have you not learned by now that I'm practically offense proof?" he asked.

"You are kind of. It's nice. You're also calm. That's a definite bonus," she said. She reached for the apple he'd sliced for her, but she didn't eat it. Instead she smoothed her finger over the skin a few times, staring thoughtfully at it. "You're taking me by surprise all over the place, Milo."

"Do tell," Milo said. He stretched out on the grass and propped his head in his hand.

"You're not what I expected."

"What did you expect?" he asked.

"Cockiness," she said. "But you're not cocky. You're pleasant and easy to be around, kind of soothing."

"You're making me sound like an ad for hand cream," he told her.

"I've been looking for a good hand cream for ages. And it's nice to be with someone easygoing. My life is busy and chaotic, both at work and with my family. Being near someone non-chaotic is comforting. You're scowling, but that was supposed to be a compliment."

"Men don't necessarily want to be thought of as soothing," he said.

"Most men probably don't, but you're not like other men," she said.

"I'm glad you're getting a chance to hit pause on your busy life, but, Jessamine," he sat up and took her hand, "I am like other men. Don't mistake calmness for something else."

"Like what?" she asked. By her tone, he could tell she was amused by him.

"Like safety. I'm not your buddy, and I'm definitely not your brother. I'm a man who is patiently waiting for the current crisis to be over because I want to be with you."

"I keep telling you I'm not interested," she said.

"You keep telling me, or you keep telling yourself?" he asked. He brought her hand closer and kissed the tender inside of her wrist.

"It's not a good time, we're not a good fit, and I'm not interested in romance right now, with you or anyone," she said. Her tone turned defensive.

"Okay," he said.

"What do you mean okay?" she asked.

"I mean okay. I can't force you into a relationship. You're a strong woman who knows her mind. All I can do is present my case to the best of my ability and hope you'll change your mind," he said.

"Are you using reverse psychology on me?" she asked.

"Only if it's working," he said. "But really, I have no desire to try and force you to be or do anything. I like you who you are, where you are."

"Where I am is at your house under lock and key," she pointed out.

"A minor technicality," he said.

She wanted to maintain her irritation with him, but it was impossible to do when he was smiling and smoothing his fingers gently on her wrist. He was attempting to bypass her defenses, and it was working, at least a little. But he underestimated how fortified her walls were. She'd been down this road before with men, the challenge phase. They wanted her because she was unattainable. And then when they attained her, they quickly realized she was much more than they'd bargained for. *Sometimes you have to let the man open the pickle jar,* her grandmother was fond of saying. But it wasn't just pickle jars Jessamine could open herself. In fact, she hadn't yet found anything she needed a man for that she wasn't capable of doing herself. It wasn't that she didn't like men. In fact, she loved men. Some of her best friends were men, including her brothers. Rather she had found that lowering her defenses and allowing a man to get too close never worked out well. Eventually they always began to resent her for something, either her capability or her busyness. In Jessamine's experience, what men seemed to want most from her was someone to fawn over them, and she had no idea how to do that. Milo's assurances that he liked her for herself were nice, but they rang false for her because she'd heard them all before.

"Can you have your list ready by tonight?" she asked.

"What list?" he asked, his face a blank.

"You said you could make me a list of other things that need done around here," she reminded him. Would he catch the challenge in her tone?

If he did, his bland smile didn't show it. "Sure, I'll try to have it finished by the time Iz gets home."

"You don't have to go get her?"

"She rides the bus home. In the morning, it's too much of an early start so I take pity on her and give her a ride," he said. His glance slid away from her, bouncing down the lane with a frown as he thought of his daughter. Jessamine didn't have to be a mind reader to wonder why. It was obvious to anyone with eyes that the girl was struggling with teenage insecurity, and possibly even depression.

"I don't know what I would have done without my dad in my life, when I was a kid. Or even now," Jessamine said.

Milo resumed his easy smile. "I hope Iz someday feels the same. Quitting my job, coming home, it seemed like such a clear cut decision. But now that I'm here, well, let's say it's a lot harder than I thought it would be. I guess I didn't realize how much of my identity was wrapped up in my job. The expression 'fish out of water' has never made so much sense before."

"I have mad respect for anyone who could quit a job to take care of family," Jessamine said.

"Yeah, mad respect?" he repeated.

"It's going to pay off, even if you can't see it right now. Family is forever. That's what my dad always told us, that we weren't just building a company, we were building our family. And that's why we don't actually fight, despite all the yelling. Because our family always comes first, before the money, before the identity, even before the newfound fame. Who cares about any of that if you don't have family to share it with? I'd give it all up in a heartbeat if I thought it was coming between me and my brothers or me and my parents."

"You really mean that, don't you?" he asked. He'd never known anyone who loved her job as much as she loved hers, and yet he believed she would walk away if she thought it was hurting her family.

"Without a second thought," she said.

"Huh," he said, staring at the grass in front of him.

"Huh, what?" she asked.

"I couldn't figure out my crazy, undue attraction to you, especially after I vowed to swear off women and relationships forever. But maybe I recognized that we're more alike than we realize because I loved my job, but I love my daughter more. People thought I was crazy to give it up, to walk away, to come back to this town with nothing in my pocket. But for Iz, it was worth it. I still believe that, and I always will, despite being unemployed and living in a hovel."

"It's not a hovel," Jessamine argued. "It's in need of some TLC."

"Aren't we all?" he said.

"Why did you swear off women and relationships forever?" she asked.

"That, Miss Samperi, is a discussion for another time. I have a list of chores to make for my handywoman, and she's kind of demanding, so I'd best not be late with it."

"You'd better keep her. Good handywomen are impossible to find these days," Jessamine said.

"Believe me, I'm working on it," he said. He kissed the top of her head and disappeared inside before she could scurry back up the ladder.

CHAPTER 20

Jessamine finished the roof in two days, mostly because she worked eighteen hours at a stretch, pausing only when Milo demanded she take a break for food. When it was finished, she felt good, the same rush of accomplishment she always felt when a job was done. There was an echo of anxiety in the feeling because she wasn't sure how to fill her time next, but Milo stuck to his word and provided her with a list. She sat at the table perusing the list and eating a piece of chocolate cake—who knew Milo could also bake?

"I'm going to need supplies," she told him. "I'll give you a list for my brothers."

"Okay," Milo said. He sat beside her at the table, drinking coffee and reading a book. He had read every night so far, proving that his book-loving high school persona hadn't been for effect. Iz was nearby on the couch, perusing the internet on a laptop. Jessamine felt wary about that. Should kids be on the internet? It seemed like there was a lot of danger lurking there, but Milo seemed unconcerned.

"Bed, Iz," he called without looking up. Iz closed the laptop and left the room. Jessamine had missed bedtime the night before because she was still on the roof, so she wasn't sure exactly what their routine was.

"You don't tuck her in?" she asked.

"She's twelve," Milo said.

"My parents tucked me in until I was eighteen and moved out. I never felt too old for it. When did she grow out of it?"

He turned his book over on the table and finally looked up. "To be honest, I have no idea. My wife always handled bedtime, mostly because I wasn't here. Do you think that's something I'm supposed to be doing?"

"Maybe you don't have to call it tucking in. Maybe it could simply be a way to check in with her, to see how her day was, to send her off to sleep with pleasant thoughts," Jessamine suggested. "Or maybe not. What do I know about kids or parenting? I just know that I liked it when I was a kid, but maybe that's because there were so many of us it seemed to be a way to have my parents' attention to myself for a bit."

"No, you're probably right, and it sounds like a good idea." He stood and held out his hand to her.

"What?"

"Come with me," he said.

"Why? I'm a stranger. She's going to think it's weird," Jessamine said.

"She's not going to think it's any weirder than having me show up. In fact, it will probably make it less weird, like it's a thing we do now because you're here. Please? I could use the moral support. Being the single dad of a twelve year old girl is not the cakewalk I make it out to be."

She put her hand in his and allowed him to lead her to Iz's bedroom, which also happened to be her bedroom. Milo knocked on the door.

"Come in," Iz said, probably thinking it was Jessamine come to retrieve her nightclothes to set out in the bathroom. She hadn't done it the night before and felt bad about waking the girl as she wrestled with her suitcase in the darkened room.

"Night, Iz," Milo said, taking a tentative step into the room.

"Night, Dad," Iz said, sounding confused. Milo lingered, and the father and daughter stared at each other in silence.

"Did you have a good day today?" Milo asked.

"Um, sure," Iz said.

"What are you reading?" Jessamine asked, noting the book on Iz's nightstand.

"It's a book I have to read for my English class," Iz said.

"Is it good?" Jessamine asked.

"Eh," Iz replied.

"Can I see it?" Jessamine asked. Without waiting for a reply, she walked farther into the room, picked the book up, and read the cover. "One time when I was in middle school, my mom got curious about what I was reading and decided to read the book for herself. She freaked out and demanded a conference with the teacher because there was so much bad language and adult material in the book. She told other parents, and they read it, and kind of freaked out, too. A petition was started to get the book removed from the list. It started this whole big thing about censorship, and I was the teacher's least favorite student from then on out. It was mortifying."

"That would be super embarrassing," Iz agreed, darting a look at Milo as if afraid they had given him some ideas.

"Yeah, it was bad, but after that my mom started reading a lot of my books out loud with me, and that was kind of fun." She also glanced at Milo who reached for the book.

"I guess that's my hint. Where are you at, Iz?"

She told him the relevant chapter, and he started to read before pausing to look at Jessamine. "Are you going to sit, or do you prefer to hover?"

She perched on the other side of Iz's bed. Milo read a few chapters, and they said goodnight to Iz. Maybe it was Jessamine's imagination, but she seemed slightly more open, a little less drawn into herself.

"You have a nice reading voice," Jessamine told him. "I have a hard time engaging in books because my mind won't be still, but listening to you read was like magic. I didn't want you to stop. I'm already looking forward to tomorrow to hear what happens next."

"I could read something else to you, if you like," he offered.

Jessamine thought of the to-do list he'd made for her. She could easily get started on it tonight. But if she did, she might run out of things to do before it was time to go home. "Sounds good."

"Do you have a preference? You can check my library, I have rather a lot of books."

"You choose, I trust you," she said.

"Good, I'll read you one of my favorites. Back in a sec, it's in my room." She seated herself on the couch, trying not to feel antsy and failing. Her fingers itched, still missing her phone. Maybe she should take up knitting or crochet to give them an outlet.

Milo returned in short order and sat close beside her on the couch. He started to read, and soon Jessamine was lost in a world of espionage and double agents. When his voice began to grow scratchy and he closed the book, it was nearly two hours later. It was possibly the longest she had ever sat still since she learned to walk as an infant.

"You're stopping there? It's a total cliffhanger," she complained.

"Now you'll have something to look forward to tomorrow night," he said.

She stretched and stopped halfway when she caught him looking at her. How was he able to do that with his eyes? He made no secret of his attraction to her, and yet it wasn't creepy or leering. It was more *adoring,* if such a thing were possible. But of course it wasn't; he barely knew her. And if he did know her, he wouldn't be adoring her. He would most likely be exasperated with her. That seemed to be the predominant emotion men felt when they got close to her.

"Tomorrow's Sunday," she said. "Samperi Sunday. I haven't missed one in a long time."

"I'm sorry you're going to miss your family day, but we'll try to make it a good one here," Milo promised.

"What did you have in mind?" Jessamine asked.

"Wait and see," Milo said, and now Jessamine found she had two things to look forward to on the morrow.

CHAPTER 21

The next morning, Jessamine woke with her usual jolt and a familiar feeling of purpose. Her mind instantly landed on the to-do list Milo had made for her. She could probably knock out half of it by sundown. But when she rolled out of bed and went to the kitchen, she saw him making waffles from scratch. It had been a long time since she had waffles. As if reading her mind, Milo also made strawberry sauce and freshly whipped cream, two of her favorites.

They ate a leisurely breakfast with Iz. Jessamine's eyes fell on the list, she reached for it, and Milo spoke. "Let's go for a walk."

"A walk? I thought I'm not supposed to go out in public," she reminded him.

"Who says we're going out in public? I own six acres. Welcome to the high life, baby," he said, spreading his hands wide to encompass the dark, dumpy kitchen.

Jessamine laughed. "All right, Daddy Warbucks, let me grab my shoes." She returned to the kitchen a few minutes later. Milo took her hand and then reached for Iz's. They set off like the three bears. If Iz found it odd that her father was holding her hand and the hand of her houseguest, she didn't let on, and neither did Jessamine. To the outside observer it would probably look like they were a family who did this every day.

They walked through the rolling green pasture behind the barn, hopped a fence—Iz needed help with that; Jessamine didn't—and entered the woods at the back of the property. At the edge of the woods was a meandering stream. Milo turned back into the little boy he had probably once been, the sort who turns over every rock in search of crawdads. He waded into the stream and began looking for whatever he could find. Jessamine, who had spent her childhood much the same, followed suit, and Iz joined them, hesitantly, as if the experience were new.

"The sky's looking dark," Milo said after a long time. "We should head back." They started for the house, but too late. The clouds opened and began a torrential downpour. They sprinted for the barn and stood under the awning, watching the storm. Jessamine couldn't remember the last time she had done anything as mundane as watch the rain, but she enjoyed it. The only thing missing was a comfortable place to perch.

"Since I got wet, can I skip my shower today?" Iz asked.

"Not a chance," Milo said, and Iz groaned. She had showered every day Jessamine had been there, but her hair still came out hanging over her face in a greasy sheet. Jessamine was beginning to have her suspicions about that.

"Iz, have you ever heard of SWAG?" Jessamine asked.

"Yeah, but I don't really know what it is," Iz said.

"It stands for Stuff We All Get. I went to a thing last month, and they gave me some SWAG. Included in the basket was some fancy shampoo and conditioner from a New York salon that cost three hundred dollars each. I brought them with me. Do you want to use them today?"

"Really?" Iz asked. She was at that difficult age where she wanted to show a teenager's disdain for everything but was still young enough to be unable to stop childish enthusiasm from leaking through.

"Sure. It's super concentrated, though, so you only need a little bit. And you only put the conditioner on the very tips of your hair." She touched the ends of Iz's hair and watched her face while she digested the information.

"Is that only because it's fancy, or are you always supposed to put conditioner on the ends?" Iz asked.

"Always only on the ends," Jessamine said.

Iz's face wore the expression again, the one that said she was thinking deep things and trying not to show it. She hadn't yet learned how to mask her emotions, however, and her face betrayed her. Jessamine had wondered if the problem wasn't a lack of washing but rather an incorrect washing technique and a slathering of conditioner all over her head. Judging by Iz's face, she had guessed correctly. Her heart broke a bit for the girl. Growing up in a family of men, she had relied heavily on her mother to teach her how to be a woman. What would her life have been like if she hadn't had a mother to guide her through the rocky teen years? Had Iz started her period yet? If so, how was Milo handling that? Had she started shaving? Would she learn how with no one to teach her? There were a million things a girl needed her mother for, Jessamine realized. She had the sudden desire to fling herself into her mother's arms and be babied and smothered as much as her mother wanted.

Milo caught her eye over Iz's head and gave her a warm smile. She had vastly underestimated how difficult his life was and how hard he was working to keep it all together. Financial hardship was only a drop in the bucket. He was trying to keep another human alive, to bring her unassisted into the adult world. How could anyone handle the weight of that alone? Before her niece was born, having children had all seemed theoretical. But after seeing the challenges Moss and Molly faced with Bella, Jessamine had started to realize how much work children actually were. She had also begun to wonder if she actually wanted them. How could anyone ever be ready for that?

What had his wife been like? Had she and Milo been supportive and loving partners, as Moss and Molly were? Had they been at war? What happened to her, and why did no one ever mention her?

The rain petered out. They walked back to the house and Jessamine retrieved her shampoo and conditioner.

"It smells so good," Iz said, opening the bottle to sniff. "It's like being at a spa."

Jessamine eyed the dark little bathroom with the tiny showerhead and thought it was nothing like a spa, but she didn't say so. "For sure. Enjoy. When you're done, I'll dry your hair, if you'd like."

"Really?" Iz asked with a pathetic amount of hopefulness. It was highly likely she realized her hair was a mess and wanted to fix it but had no idea how. Jessamine remembered the hopelessness of that age, of feeling like things were bad and would never get better. In her case, she'd been mortified by her too-big nose. But she'd also had a loving, supportive mother and family to help her shake it off and move on. Iz had no one but Milo.

She smiled and leaned in, whispering. "Maybe we could also test out some of my makeup, if you promise not to tell your dad." She put her finger to her lips.

Iz nodded enthusiastically before bounding off to take her shower.

When Jessamine arrived in the kitchen, she found Milo brewing a pot of coffee. "I hope there's enough in there for two," she said. She was a coffee snob who owned an expensive Italian espresso machine and used only imported beans she ground fresh every day in an equally expensive burr grinder. Milo owned a twenty dollar coffee pot and used a can of generic grounds. The taste was different, but the effect was the same: sweet, precious caffeine.

He finished preparing the coffee and turned, enveloping her in a big hug. The kitchen was so tiny he didn't have to take any steps to get to her. "Thanks for being kind to my kid. You're nice," he said, resting his head on hers.

"She's a sweet kid," Jessamine said, returning his hug. He released her, and she took a step back. "I have a list for you to give to my brothers, of things I need or want. And I want you to grab my toolbox from my house."

"Is my toolbox not good enough for you?" he teased.

"You're actually calling a hammer and four mismatched screws a toolbox?" she said.

"There are a few nails, too," he defended.

"Those are nails? I thought that was your rust collection," she said.

"Yes, but you should see my measuring cups." He kissed his fingers and released them, and she laughed. If she were being honest, she found him a bit fascinating. He was hopeless at home repair, fainted at the mere thought of heights, and baked one of the best chocolate cakes she'd ever tasted. But he was also comfortable with a gun and would literally give his life to protect her. Her brain was having trouble classifying him into any quantifiable category. The more she got to know him, the less she seemed to know him. His open, gregarious demeanor was a cover for a lot of mystery.

"I'm not sure why you're looking at me like that, but it's making my little heart go pitty-pat," Milo said.

"What exactly was your job in the military?" she asked.

"A little of this, a little of that," he said.

"You say you're an open book, but I've asked you a lot of questions, and you've never given me a straight answer to any of them," she noted.

"Haven't I?" He smiled in a way that made *her* heart go pitty-pat.

"I'd like to see your squeaky floorboard," she said.

"Is that some kind of contractor innuendo?" he asked.

She picked up the list of chores he'd made for her. "Your squeaky floorboard."

"Ah, right. Follow me to my room." He led her down the hall. "When I bought this house, I noticed the squeak. I asked the sellers to swap out the floorboard, and they assured me they did." He opened the door for her and allowed her to precede him inside.

"They probably did," Jessamine said. She tested the sagging board a few times, cocking her head each time it squeaked.

"If they fixed it, why is it not fixed?" Milo asked.

"Because the problem isn't in the floorboard. The problem is in the joist below; it's sagging. You had termites, yes?"

"Not personally," he said. "But, yes, the house had them when I bought it. They were supposedly treated."

"They were," Jessamine assured him.

"How could you possibly know these things? Can you also tell me my horoscope?"

"I did a perimeter check before I went on the roof. I saw the termite tunnels. The good news is that they're dormant. The bad news is that they likely got to your joists and did some damage."

"That sounds bad," Milo said. *And expensive.*

Jessamine shrugged unconcernedly. "Depends on how long they were allowed to fester. It could be that only this joist is bad, in which case I'll jack up the floor beneath us and replace it."

"What if it's all the joists?" he asked.

"Then I'll grab my stuff and run out of here before the house collapses," she said.

"Thank you, that was a soothing answer," he said.

She laughed. "It's not a big deal. I've encountered termites before."

"I don't need your dating history," he said. "How can you possibly know all these things?"

"My dad started teaching me at a young age, and I was an eager pupil. Your dad wasn't handy, I take it."

"He was, actually, but he died when I was three. I was raised by my mom and five sisters who were, not surprisingly based on how I turned out, not handy at all," he said.

"I had no idea your dad died. I'm so sorry." He'd had a lot of tragedy in his life. Her eyes strayed to the table beside the bed and a picture of a woman and baby, presumably his wife and Iz. Jessamine opened her mouth to ask when Iz appeared in the doorway.

"What are you guys doing?" she asked.

"Talking about bugs," Milo said.

Iz wrinkled her nose. "Gross, why?"

"Jessamine's known, and apparently dated, a lot of them," Milo said.

"I'm finished with my shower," Iz said, her eyes landing hopefully on Jessamine.

"Great, let me grab my stuff," Jessamine said.

"What stuff?" Milo asked.

"It's a secret. Girls only," Jessamine said.

"You can't keep secrets from me in my own house," he said with enough mock indignation to make Iz giggle.

"I can if I go up on the roof. I could hide anything up there," Jessamine said.

"Low blow, Samperi," Milo said.

Jessamine tossed him a kiss as she left the room, followed by Iz who imitated her with the same gesture.

"Don't teach her to flirt," Milo called, and was rewarded by the sound of Iz's giggle, something he'd heard far too little of the last couple of years.

CHAPTER 22

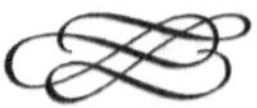

The next morning when Milo returned from taking Iz to school, he couldn't find Jessamine again. Unconcerned this time, he eventually located her sitting under the overhang of the barn, drinking coffee as she stared out at the horseless pasture.

"It's such a pretty view," she commented as he joined her and sat down.

"What am I sitting on?" he asked.

"A bench," she said.

"Where'd it come from?" he asked, hanging his head between his knees to check it out.

"I made it."

"When?" he asked.

"This morning. I would have made a chair, but I could only find enough lumber scraps in the barn for this bench," she said, taking another sip of coffee.

"I can't believe you built a bench without a chair. You are such a hopeless, lazy slacker. By the way, I picked up all the stuff you wanted and your brothers say hello. They said to give you this note." He reached into his pocket and delivered the letter.

She reached for the note and read it, smiling. "This is the longest I've ever been away from my family."

"How are you holding up?" Milo asked.

"Better than expected. You have this image of yourself, that you're tough and independent, and then you begin to wonder if maybe it's because you've never been tested. I've never been away from my family, never been truly on my own. What does that say about me?"

"That you are loved," he assured her. "I've lived away from my family for most of my life. The only difference between the person I was when I was halfway across the world and the person I am now is that I have somewhere to go on the holidays. Your foundation will always be with you, no matter where you take it." He reached for her coffee, and she handed it over, allowing him to take a sip.

"What happened to your wife?"

He coughed, sputtering his mouthful of coffee.

"You can keep that now, by the way," she said, grimacing at the mug as he wiped his chin.

"It's a long story," Milo said after he recovered.

She rested her hand on his knee. "Milo, I need to know, and I feel like maybe you need to talk about it."

He drew in a deep breath and held it a few beats before letting go. "Have you ever talked to a divorced person who made their ex sound like Satan? Like everything was the ex's fault and you knew that couldn't be possible because there are always, always two sides? I've never wanted to be that person. So I'll start by telling you I was a lousy husband, at least in the beginning. We married young, and we've already established that I was immature and stupid. I was also completely self-centered and convinced of my rightness in every circumstance. Christine and I fought a lot, and a good portion of that fighting was my fault. Our future looked grim, and then Iz arrived." He paused, smiling. "That was a game changer. Becoming a father, combined with the maturing effect of being a marine, made me realize how much I wanted my family to work. But I was gone a lot, so much."

He paused again and took another sip of coffee. Jessamine didn't rush him. He'd get there when he was ready.

He took a breath and began again. "Being in a military family isn't easy—the separation, the constant uncertainty of the future, the recurring moves as soon as you begin to get settled. Christine was especially sensitive to the strain of everything. I began to realize that what I had first discounted as moodiness in the early years was something more serious. Having Iz seemed to exacerbate everything that was going on with her. I'll say this for her—she tried her best to be a good mother. But it was as if that was all she could do. She saw Iz off to school in the morning, and then existed until she arrived home again. She didn't go out, didn't cook, didn't clean, didn't even shower most days. I know this because I was so worried that I asked friends to check in on her while I was away. And then when I came home, it was as if she could release Iz to my care and completely cocoon herself away from us.

"I tried to get her help, I swear to you I tried. When she refused to see a counselor, therapist or doctor, I asked the base chaplain to stop by, but she refused to see him, too. She had no friends, no family to speak of."

He stopped again, staring off into the distance without really seeing anything. Jessamine smoothed her thumb comfortingly over his knee. He took her hand and twined his fingers through hers, and that seemed to give him the courage to go on.

"When I got the call that Christine wrapped her car around a tree, seemingly intentionally, and she was gone, we thought Iz was with her. It wasn't until hours later I learned that Iz had gone home with a friend that day. For a few hours, I thought I lost them both. You can't imagine what that was like. When I realized I still had Iz, I quit that minute. Of course, being the military, it wasn't that easy, but my decision was made. I needed to be with my daughter."

Jessamine thought that was the end, but he took a breath and continued. "I thought I would have a few months to concentrate on Iz, to find another job. We had a healthy amount in savings. But when I arrived home and began cleaning up, I realized Christine had developed a gambling habit. Not only had she drained our savings, but she had racked up an enormous amount of debt. It was hard, and I had a lot of anger. I swore, *swore* I would never get involved with anyone else again, or at least not until Iz left home. And then I saw this woman, sitting at a bar." He gave her a smile and squeezed her hand.

"Let me remind you we're not involved," she said, though she made no move to withdraw her hand.

"So you say," he replied mildly, tipping back the mug to finish the rest of her coffee.

"I'm sorry it's been so difficult for you the last couple of years— your wife's death, the transition of leaving the military, the stress of moving and trying to find a job, raising Iz on your own. You've had a lot on your plate."

"It hasn't all been bad. I'm back among family now, and my sisters and mom have been helpful to watch Iz. I have some feelers out, as far as a job goes. And recently I reconnected with a woman I met when I was seventeen. We danced together at homecoming my senior year. It was epic."

"It was an epic failure," she corrected.

"Why did you ask me to dance?" he asked.

"Because I was fourteen and didn't know better," she said.

"Because you had a crush on me. Admit it, woman." He squeezed her hand.

"Fine, I had a crush on you, but it died that night. I spent the rest of the year secretly loathing you. By the time graduation rolled around, I was researching how to do voodoo curses."

"And now all these years later, you're still trying to loathe me. And failing, I might add," he said.

"You're awfully full of yourself," she accused.

"No, I'm not. Jess, I get it. You're beautiful, talented, accomplished, confident, wealthy, and famous. I'm a dead broke, jobless, single father who lives in a rundown heap. Materially, I have nothing to offer you. On paper, it's a terrible match from your point of view. But in here." He used his free hand to tap his heart. "It all makes sense. I could make you happy; I could love you the way you need to be loved. I don't know how I know, but I know. You might not see it right now, but we work."

She shook her head.

"Why don't you believe me?" he demanded.

"Because I know me. There's this gaping, clawing chasm inside me that always wants more. I want to be more, do more, I want more out of life, and I want more from the person I'm with. I've tried to date before, some good guys, some spectacular guys. But I couldn't settle down, couldn't rest, couldn't let go of that part of me that was always reaching for something better. I like you. You're a good guy. We have fun together, and you're stupid handsome. And that's why I don't want to see me happen to you. Some people aren't meant to settle down, to have a long-term relationship. I'm one of those people."

"You're breaking my heart," he said

"You'll get over me. Quickly."

"You're breaking my heart for you. How can you talk about yourself like that? How could you consider withholding love from yourself because you believe you're too much for someone?"

"Past experience is a good teacher," she said. "I've been interested in men before, and they've been interested in me, but it always ends the same. They end up resenting my job, and I end up resenting them for trying to take me away from my job."

"What bothers me is how little that bothers you," Milo said. "I get that you're driven and ambitious, that you love to work and you love your job, but you're not a robot, you're not a machine. You have a heart, a huge, beautiful heart, and it's going to waste."

"It's not going to waste. I love my family, I love my friends. I'm just not comfortable with the idea of myself as a wife or mother."

"What do you think being a wife or mother entails that you're not prepared for?" he asked.

"Giving up too much of myself, giving my time, energy, identity."

"If you think that, why did you wake early to do Iz's hair this morning, why did you help her with her outfit?"

"I was being nice. She's clearly struggling with some things right now, I thought it would give her a perk to feel pretty and put together today."

"Why did you get her cereal for her when I was in the shower?" he asked.

"She was still half asleep and running late. It wasn't a big deal."

"Why are you sitting here talking to me right now?" he asked.

"What are you talking about? We're having a conversation," she said.

"Exactly," he said, his tone triumphant.

"Exactly what?" she asked. "I have no idea what you're saying."

"I'm saying that those moments, doing a kid's hair, getting her breakfast, sitting down to have a conversation, are what being a wife and mother are all about."

She rolled her eyes. "You're being ridiculous. It's not the same at all."

"It's exactly the same, it's just a whole lot more of those same kinds of moments all rolled together."

"What about being pregnant, going into labor, giving birth, feeding a newborn at four in the morning, arguing over whose turn it is to take the dog out or do the laundry, fussing about how much money was spent buying clothes or bickering over who gets to drive the good car and which music to listen to while you're driving?" she asked. "Don't pretend that doing your kid's hair one morning or getting her a bowl of cereal makes me a mother anymore than this conversation makes us husband and wife."

"Of course that's not what I'm saying, but my point is the same. Being a mother is hard work, but it doesn't come at you all at once. It comes at you a moment at a time, like losing sleep to fix hair or getting a kid's cereal before you've had your coffee. And marriage is the same. It's not a big, overwhelming relationship. It's a whole bunch of little moments like these, sitting side by side on the porch and talking things through, one conversation at a time. Sometimes it's hard and maddening, draining, and exhausting. But it's also a rewarding, fulfilling, explosion of joy. You want to think about the bad—the labor, the sleepless nights—let me tell you the good, staring at a baby at four in the morning as she drinks milk your body made for her, knowing she's yours, that you created her in a mad rush of love. You want to talk about arguments over taking the dog out—let me tell you about picking out that puppy together, of lying twined together at night talking over your day in intimate whispers. If you don't want all the bad parts of motherhood and marriage, that's fine. But don't pretend you won't also be giving up all the bliss that goes with it."

Jessamine stood. "Is my stuff in your car?"

"What stuff?" he asked.

"The stuff you picked up for me this morning?"

He blinked up at her, his mind trying to play catch up. He wanted to say more, Jessamine could tell. With effort, he stuffed down his reply and nodded.

She turned and stalked toward the house, intending to get started on her list, but the conversation with Milo kept trying to intrude. What if he was right? What if being in a relationship could simply be an extension of who she already was? But, no, she was sure he was wrong because it had never happened to her before. Everyone she had ever dated had tried to change her, to get her to be more attentive, less capable, more nurturing. She was certain Milo would too, if he ever really got to know her.

CHAPTER 23

Over the next few days, Jessamine completed the list Milo made for her. She fixed the sagging floorboard in his room by jacking up the floor and marrying a new joist to the damaged one. He was having a problem with his furnace and air conditioner. HVAC repair wasn't Jessamine's specialty by any stretch, but Moss was a certified installer. After a few back and forth messages with him, she was able to figure out the problem and get it fixed. She replaced the bathroom and kitchen faucets, adding a garbage disposal while she had everything torn out. At some point the kitchen sink had leaked, causing significant damage to the base of the cabinet beneath it, so she ripped that portion out and replaced it with new wood.

During these times, Milo sat on the floor beside her, handing her tools and making conversation. "Do you ever feel like you're putting lipstick on a pig?" he asked.

"More like artificial limbs. It may not make a difference in the appearance of things, but your function is going to be a lot better here," she replied. She fixed the squeaky front door and the saggy back door and replaced the locks on both. "You never changed them after you bought the house? That's the first thing you're supposed to do," she chided.

"It's fine, I feel pretty secure here," he said. He still hadn't told her about the safeguards he'd set up around the perimeter.

She put new gaskets around both doors, something Milo hadn't even known existed until she showed him how his were failing. "That will help keep it warm this winter," she explained before turning her attention to the windows. Ideally he needed replacement windows. Barring that, Jessamine did the next best thing by removing each one and putting in new insulation and caulking, fixing the sag and stopping the whistling wind from streaming in.

After that the list was finished and she began finding new things to do that he hadn't even thought of. One day she put the front loader on his tractor and began digging dirt away from the foundation. He had no idea what that was about until she unearthed large pieces of drainage tile, stacked them in a tidy heap, re-graded the entire foundation, and reburied them.

"You need new gutters, but that should help stop the basement leakage," she told him, and he nodded as if he had any idea his basement was leaking or how the gutters had an effect on that.

When she finished with the re-grading, she made a chair to go with the bench she'd made. When the chair was finished, she made a porch swing. As she was hanging the porch swing, she found more termite damage on the porch and spent a day repairing and painting.

After she finished with the porch, Milo couldn't possibly imagine what else she would come up with. And then he walked into the bathroom and found the entire shower torn out.

"I was only going to put up a new shower head, but whoever tiled this the first time was a moron. No vapor barrier. I mean seriously..." she trailed off in disgust and resumed removing tile. He didn't ask where they would shower the next few days because, knowing her, it would be done before he could blink. She sent another note to her brothers and, in no time, the back of his car was loaded with a shower pan, mastic, subway tile, and the largest shower head he had ever seen. He had long since given up trying to protest the cost or wonder who was paying for everything.

By the next day, the shower was finished—mostly because

Jessamine stayed up all night tiling. Literally the whole night. Milo had gotten up twice to check on her. The third time he appeared, she snapped at him.

"I'm fine, stop looking concerned. This isn't the first time I've stayed up all night tiling." In answer, he picked her up and locked her out of the room so he could use the toilet.

"Oops, sorry," she said, giving him a sheepish smile as he stumbled blindly back to his bed.

Iz's squeal of delight startled him awake the next morning. He stumbled back to the bathroom and inspected Jessamine's handiwork.

"It's like a spa," Iz said, clapping her hands together in excitement. "A for real spa."

"Yes, it is," Jessamine said definitively, draping her arm around Iz's shoulders. Iz leaned into her slightly, hungry for further affection. Milo put his arms around them both.

"It is by far the best part of the house now," Milo agreed. The shower was shiny and trendy, pure white subway tile with a foot-wide showerhead that came directly out of the ceiling. A shower would feel exactly like standing in warm and gentle rainstorm.

"Can I have Maisy over to look at it?" Iz asked.

Milo and Jessamine made eye contact over Iz's head. "Who's Maisy?" Milo asked.

"One of my friends," Iz replied in what he called her patented *duh, Dad* tone.

Jessamine and Milo looked at each other again. As far as they knew, this was her first friend. "You want to bring someone over to stare at our shower?" Milo teased. "She must be really hard up for entertainment."

"Or this is a particularly spectacular shower," Jessamine suggested.

"It is that," Milo agreed, giving her hand a squeeze behind Iz's back.

"Are you guys going to let me go?" Iz asked, a token protest since she was clearly enjoying the hug.

"We're making an Iz sandwich," Milo said.

"Dad," Iz intoned. "You never answered about Maisy."

"Not right now, but maybe after Jess is gone," Milo said, and the atmosphere in the room cooled immediately.

"Why does she have to go?" Iz mumbled, squirming free of their embrace.

"This was only ever temporary, Iz," Milo said.

"But I still live in town. We'll still see each other; we'll still be friends," Jess assured her.

Iz nodded, still looking morose.

"My sister-in-law, Lou, has an amazing pool. We'll go swimming sometime," Jessamine promised. "You can bring Maisy or anyone else."

Iz perked up. "Really?"

"Absolutely, and my parents have horses. They're gentle and love to be ridden. We'll go for a long ride."

"Really?" Iz repeated, her eyes bugging.

"As long as it's okay with your dad," Jessamine remembered to add.

Iz turned hopefully to him. "Well, I don't know," he drawled.

"Dad," she intoned, somehow making the word into four syllables. "I'm going to go message Maisy and tell her."

"Don't mention Jessamine or the Samperis," Milo reminded her. "Just say you have a friend who invited you to do that stuff. Got it, Iz? Do not mention Jess or the Samperis."

"Dad, I've got it. I'm not stupid," she said in the same longsuffering tone. She wriggled out of the room. Milo closed the gap she had vacated, snuggling Jessamine deep into his embrace.

"She never acted like that before you came along and put ideas in her head about doing her hair and makeup and wearing clothes that match." Among the other things Jessamine had brought into the house, new clothes and shoes for Iz had been among them, though Milo thought her sisters-in-law and mother had more to do with the selection than her brothers who seemed confused about how the items had ended up in their possession. She had made a startling transformation after Jessamine taught her how to wash and style her hair. The added confidence in her appearance seemed to be the boost she needed to reach out to other kids. "You made my baby an actual teenager, and now I think you owe me."

"Yeah? What do I owe you?" she asked. Her face tipped up to his as her arms snaked around his neck. As the days passed, it became harder to stay away from each other, though they hadn't given in to temptation entirely. Mostly there had been a few stolen moments of affection, as now. Usually Jessamine was too busy for anything more, a bonus since Milo seemed unable to stay away from her.

"A new baby," he said.

"Ha," she puffed a loud laugh, more from shock than amusement. "Going for the gold, aren't you?"

"I believe in aiming high," he said. "If you shoot for the sun, you still might hit the moon."

"What would the moon be, in this case?" she asked.

"Anything with you is a moon landing," he said.

She pressed impossibly closer, her fingers sliding into his hair. "Milo, so handsome," she mused, her eyes roaming his face with approval.

"Does tiling often have this effect on you?" he asked.

"Or possibly it's the fact that I haven't slept in two days and I'm highly caffeinated."

"In that case, I'm going to build a sleep-deprivation chamber and stock the fridge with Red Bull," he said. "Hey, thank you for fixing my house and my kid. What you've been able to accomplish here has been miraculous, on both counts."

"Why does this feel like a benediction?" Jessamine asked.

"Because yesterday when I went to pick up stuff from your brothers, they gave me this note." He let go of her to fish in his pocket and hand her a slip of paper. "You were so busy last night, I saved it until today."

"A TV appearance in New York, and the network wants all of us there," she said, skimming the note.

"I know, I shamelessly read it," he said.

"Two days," she added.

He nodded.

"I take it you're not planning to bring me back here when we return," she said.

"It's been almost two weeks. Much as I'd like to, I can't keep you here forever. You have a life to get back to, as you've pointed out repeatedly. And the longer this goes on, the more chance you have of being found here. I can't risk Iz's safety like that." He let out a breath. "But I am going with you to New York." He waited a few beats for her to respond. When she didn't, he continued. "No argument?"

"You think I'd go to New York without my bodyguard? Whitney Houston taught me better than that," she said.

"I'm going to miss you a ridiculous amount. I love how I can gauge the difficulty of the day's agenda based on what you do with your hair. Leave it down—simple faucet replacement. Put it up—here come the power tools. And I absolutely adore seeing you in my flannels."

"I should have brought more work clothes," she lamented.

He shook his head. "Seeing you in mine is way better." His toe clipped the door, pushing it closed.

"What's happening?" she asked, though she was smiling.

"I'm going to pick you up, and you're five ten, so I'm going to need the support of the door." He picked her up, wrapping her legs around his waist as he pressed her against the door.

"Now what?" she asked.

"I'm going to kiss you, and you're going to like it," he said.

"I'll be the judge of that," Jessamine said. His lips barely skimmed hers when Iz knocked on the door.

"What are you guys doing? Are you trying the new shower without me?"

Milo closed his eyes. "Yep, we're busted." He reached out a hand and turned on the shower before letting Jessamine go and opening the door for Iz.

"So cool," Iz gushed, poking her head inside. "Do you think it will feel like rain?"

"One way to know for sure," Milo said. He took her hand and Jessamine's hand and herded everyone under the spray.

"It does feel like rain," Iz said. "Hey since I'm getting wet now can I..."

"No, this does not count as your shower," Milo said. "But speaking of rain." He made a checkmark over Iz's head.

"Rain V?" Jessamine guessed, smiling.

"Check, Jess, rain check. The biggest one ever," he said.

"We'll see," Jessamine said.

"We Greeks are incredibly serious about rain checks," Milo told her.

"We are?" Iz asked.

"Only Greek men," Milo amended, patting her shoulder. "Don't test it, Jess."

"Or what?" she asked, blinking excess water from her long lashes.

"Or I'll collect when you least want me to," he promised.

"When would that be?" she asked.

"I haven't been to a Samperi Sunday in a few weeks," he mused.

"You're shameless," Jessamine said.

"Shameless when it comes to loving you," Milo said.

"You love Jess, Dad?"

"That's a line from a song, honey," Milo explained.

"How does that song go again?" Jessamine prompted.

"Are you asking me to sing?" Milo clarified.

"No, Dad, no, he can't sing," Iz added, turning imploringly to Jessamine.

"What are you talking about? I'm an amazing singer," Milo said and began loudly singing an off-key rendition of *Shameless*.

Iz pressed her palms over her ears. "I told you he's horrible," she said when the song was finished.

"I don't know, Iz. I kind of liked it," Jessamine said. She was pressed in a tiny shower with lukewarm water soaking her clothes, being serenaded by a man whose voice sounded like an injured walrus bellowing for help, and she more than liked it. She kind of loved it.

CHAPTER 24

There was one more thing Jessamine wanted to accomplish before she left Milo's house, and she decided to let Iz help.

"You're going to let me paint?" Iz asked, her voice uncertain.

"Absolutely," Jessamine said. "Painting's not so hard. I'll do the trim and you can roll."

"What can I do?" Milo asked, hovering at the edge of Iz's bedroom.

"Stay over there where I can see you," Jessamine said.

"You tip over one paint can, and everyone loses their minds," Milo said.

"Painting makes me hungry for chocolate," Jessamine hinted.

"Are you using me for my baking skills?" he asked.

"Absolutely," she answered, unconcerned.

"Just so we're clear," Milo said. He turned toward the kitchen and went to prepare the cake. Meanwhile Iz and Jessamine painted Iz's bedroom.

"It kind of looks the same," Iz said, standing back to admire their work. "Except cleaner."

"Ivory's a subtle color. Tomorrow while you're at school, I'll finish, and you'll be able to see all the color variations," Jessamine promised.

"I wish I could stay home tomorrow and watch you work," Iz said.

"The magic isn't in watching the process; it's in seeing the final result," Jessamine said.

"Yeah, but I just like doing stuff with you," Iz said.

"We'll see each other again, Iz. I promise," Jessamine said. "And next time you won't have to share your room."

"But I liked sharing my room with you. Sleeping by myself all the time is lonely." She looked up as inspiration struck. "If you married my dad, you could have more kids. You could give me a brother or sister."

"Your dad and I aren't exactly dating," Jessamine said.

"Don't you like him?"

"I like him."

"Don't you think he's handsome? Girls at school think so. I even heard a couple of teachers say it once," Iz confided.

Jessamine could only imagine. "Yes, I think he's handsome."

"If you like him, and you think he's handsome, why don't you marry him?" Iz prodded.

All of a sudden Jessamine realized Milo was leaning in the door-frame. "Would you like to field this one?" she asked him.

"She's doing fine, and I'm curious to hear the answer, too," he said.

"Sometimes it's not so simple. I'm sure there have been boys you liked and thought were cute, but you didn't marry them," Jessamine said.

"I'm twelve," Iz reminded her, and Milo snickered.

"Your dad and I are friends," Jessamine pronounced, relieved to have found an out. "Grown-ups can be friends without marrying each other."

"But Dad wants to marry you, don't you?" Iz asked, turning to face Milo.

"I do," Milo said, his tone disconcertingly solemn and sincere.

"That leaves it up to you again," Iz said. "Don't you want to marry him? He's a good husband. He was really nice to my mom. He brought her flowers and presents every time he came home from deployment." She moved closer to Milo and tucked her hand in his.

Jessamine stared at the heartbreaking picture they made—the

widower and the almost orphan. "Iz, I like your dad, I really do, but I'm not ready to be married right now."

Iz opened her mouth, probably to ask why, but Milo squeezed her hand. "Enough, Iz. We have Jess's answer. You can't force someone to do something, no matter how much you want them to. You love them where they are, for who they are, and take what they can give. Jess is our friend, and that's a wonderful thing. Speaking of friends, I heard the laptop ding with a message from Maisy." Iz skittered by him, leaving Milo and Jessamine alone.

"You couldn't have jumped in with a rescue a little sooner?" she asked.

"I've tried every other avenue, so I kind of wanted to see if it would work," he said. "It had a good chance of working. Iz is relentless when she sets her mind."

"I can't imagine where she gets it," Jessamine replied.

Milo grasped her wrist and pulled her closer. "You have paint freckles all over your face." His hands migrated to her hips while hers slid around his neck, drawing him slightly closer.

"This is not going to help your daughter's confusion about the status of our relationship," Jessamine said.

"The internet is parenting her now. She's lost to us for the rest of the night," Milo replied. "Now, about that rain check."

"Samperis keep short balances," she said. This time she was the aggressor, but she had barely touched her lips to his when Iz called down the hall.

"Hey, Jess is in the news. Guys, come look."

They froze and reluctantly pulled apart. "I don't think she realizes that if we did get married, we would find it nearly impossible to give her the requested brother or sister," Milo said.

"Between us, our parents have eleven children. Where there's a will, there's a way," Jessamine said, brushing by him to head toward Iz.

"You're leaving me on that note?" Milo complained.

She turned her head to toss him a wink, and he stumbled after her, groaning.

"What's wrong with Dad?" Iz asked.

"Old people problems," Jessamine said.

"More like old man problems," Milo agreed. Jessamine was already sitting beside Iz. He picked her up and set her in his lap, taking her place beside Iz. "What are they saying about our Jess, Iz?"

"It's all about how she's in hiding because someone is stalking her. I didn't know that was why she was here. You just said she was in danger," Iz said accusingly to Milo.

"You're twelve. I didn't think you needed every detail," Milo replied.

She huffed and continued scrolling the article. "There's a bunch of stuff about how no one has seen her and no one knows where she's hiding." She peered closer at the computer. "They don't mention you at all, Dad."

"That's kind of the point, hon," Milo said. "It's my job to remain anonymous and unseen. Actually, I'm impressed they've kept it quiet this long. I wonder how it got out." He looked at Jessamine to gauge her reaction and saw her reading the comments at the bottom of the screen. He returned his attention to the compute.

It's a wonder she can see to design anything beyond that giant schnoz.

Maybe she's hiding under a giant tissue.

Man, I find her so annoying, and her designs are tacky and cheap.

I hate all the Samperis. So fake and annoying.

Fake Brooklyn accents plus fake Kentucky accents equal lose/lose.

Of course she has a stalker. Attention hog much? Eye roll.

She has to have a stalker because no one sane would want her.

Milo closed the laptop.

"Hey, I wasn't done reading," Iz protested.

"Bed, Iz," Milo said.

"But…" Iz began, but he preempted her.

"Are you going to test out the new shower or what?" Milo asked, and she dashed toward the bathroom. He waited until she was fully gone before saying more.

"You don't actually believe those things people say do you, Jess?" he asked.

"No, of course not," Jessamine said, her robotic tone doing nothing to convince him.

"They're trolls, mean, nasty trolls who think they're safe because they're anonymous. They would never have the courage to lie to someone's face like that because they know they'd probably get punched. I swear, social media brings out the absolute worst in people sometimes," Milo groused.

"I know," Jessamine said, nodding. "I should go clean my paint-brushes." She tried to stand, but he held her back.

"Let me see your face," he demanded.

She shook her head, ducking it as she pressed it to his chest. He used his hand to tip it and found her eyes streaming, lip quivering.

"Ah, Jess," he whispered, letting her face go so he could hug her tightly. She returned the hug, pressing her face back into his chest as she cried hard for a few minutes. When he felt she'd cried herself out, he spoke again.

"Look at me for a minute," he said. Her eyes were watery, but she complied, sniffling a little. He handed her a tissue, and she wiped her nose. "Don't you think I'm gorgeous?"

She laughed at the unexpected question. "Yes," she said, her voice quavery.

"And we've already established that I'm ridiculously shallow. Do you really think a guy who looks like me would be killing myself to try and be with a woman who is anything but physical perfection?" he asked.

"Milo," she breathed, resting her head on his shoulder again.

"Jessamine, it's imperative to me that you understand how unbe-lievably beautiful you are," he said. "You are the stuff dreams are made of, especially my dreams. Even the ones when I'm awake."

"I don't have low self-esteem, not really," she said. "But sometimes when I read words like that, I'm suddenly back to being that fourteen-year-old girl with the too-big hair and the too-big nose and the too-wide mouth."

"I love your big, crazy hair. It's like it's alive and has its own personality, based on the weather. When I see you emerge from your room and it can barely fit through the doorway, I know it must be humid and I should turn up the AC," he said, and she giggled. Geez, he loved when she did that. "Your nose is exactly the size it should be to compete with the rest of your face. Do you understand what you'd look like with those inch long lashes and a tiny nose? You'd be like a pug." She laughed again, harder this time. "And that mouth, ugh. You have no idea. Sometimes I ask you stupid, mundane questions so I can watch it say things."

"Oh, that's why you ask so many stupid, mundane questions," she said, but her voice sounded lighter, happier.

"Yes, I'm actually quite intelligent and well-spoken, but I've fooled you into believing I'm a bumbling moron who knocks over paint cans and faints at the sight of ladders, just so I can watch your mouth move."

She tipped her face up and enunciated her words, drawing out the syllables so he could watch her mouth work. "You're so incredibly selfless, Milo Eliopoulos."

"Have mercy," Milo whispered, and then they were kissing with no idea of who made the first move. Maybe it was him, maybe it was her, but more than likely it was mutual.

"Guys, I'm finished. Aren't you going to tuck me in? Guys?" Iz called.

"Minute," Milo said, reluctantly disentangling himself from Jessamine. He cleared his throat and tried again. "Be there in a minute."

"How *do* our parents have so many kids?" he wondered as he stood and led the way to Iz's room.

"I don't know about yours, but the traffic noises in Brooklyn are conveniently loud," Jessamine said. They reached Iz's room, and she turned to face him. "Oh, I almost forgot to tell you. When we go to New York, we're staying with my Nonna. In Brooklyn." She patted his chest and walked by him, leaving him speechless in the hallway.

CHAPTER 25

"I feel deceived." Milo and Jessamine lay on the floor of her grandmother's living room, facing each other, their hands tucked beneath their cheeks.

"Why's that?" Jessamine whispered.

"When you said we'd be staying with your grandmother in Brooklyn, I wasn't aware we'd be sharing the space with them." He pointed over his shoulder to where her four brothers lay, snoring softly.

"Was this not what you had in mind?" she asked, feigning innocence.

"We've spent the last two weeks interrupted at every turn by my daughter and, when I think we're about to finally score some alone time, we end up sharing a cubicle with your brothers," he complained. The hint of a smile in his tone told her his indignation was also feigned.

"Big families. What are you going to do?" she asked, shrugging.

"We'll have to make the best of it, I guess," he said. He reached for her hand and clasped it. The day had been long and exhausting. After seeing Iz off to school, Jessamine finished decorating her room—hanging new curtains and pictures, rearranging the furniture and adding new bedding and a couple of plants. They barely had enough time to see Iz's post-school reaction before they dropped her at Milo's sister's house and left for the airport. They flew to New York and took a taxi to Jessamine's grandmother's apartment where her brothers and a hot meal were waiting for them. The next day would be no less busy and exhausting. They should be sleeping, but instead they lay side by side, whispering like teenagers at a sleepover.

"I love that you're about to appear on a television show with four million adoring viewers, and you spend the night before sleeping on your grandmother's floor," Milo said.

"If Nonna knew we were local and didn't stay with her, she'd skin our hides," Jessamine said.

"I believe it," Milo said. "I paused eating for about ten seconds to chew, and she asked me if my eyes were too big for my stomach."

"Everyone's a member of the Clean Plate Club at Nonna's," Jessamine said. "Or else."

"Guerrilla feeding tactics," Milo said.

"Exactly. She'll also start plying you with guilt before you've even started. 'What's the matter, you don't like it? You only took one helping. Are you sick? Is it not good? Too much salt.' So you say, 'I like it, Nonna, I like it,' and add two more helpings that you'll then be forced to eat. And when you think your stomach might explode, she brings out dessert and you find you miraculously have room."

"That cake was amazing," Milo said.

"I like your cake better. Shh, our secret." She pressed her finger lightly to his lips. He kissed her finger and she smoothed it along his cheek, stopping at his dimple.

"The dreams I used to have about this dimple," she said.

"Used to?" he said.

"When I was a kid. You were my first crush," she informed him.

"You're my last crush," he said.

She blinked at him, not knowing how to respond.

"You should sleep, you have a big day tomorrow," he added.

"You should sleep, too," she said.

"I'm keeping watch," he said.

"On what?" she asked.

"Your face," he said.

"Geez, this guy is good," Moss whispered, and the other brothers snickered, albeit in whispers so as not to disturb their sleeping grandmother. "Is it working, Jess?"

"Mind your business," Jessamine whispered.

"When you're sleeping a foot away, it's all our business," Giovanni said. "It's like when Joe and Peaches were in high school and used to sneak middle of the night makeout sessions."

"You guys knew about that?" Joe said.

"You're six feet and forty five inches, Goliath. Not exactly good at tiptoeing. I'm pretty sure you stepped on my face once," Moss replied.

"Probably not an accident," Giovanni added.

"You were an annoying kid sometimes," Benny added.

"It's nice how you said 'were' and 'sometimes,'" Giovanni said.

"I was adorable. And I was the king of sneaking," Moss said.

"You mean like when you used to eat cannoli in the middle of the night?" Jessamine said.

"You knew about that?" Moss asked.

"Moss, you know we counted cannoli like precious gold coins. Do you really think none of us questioned how three of them would go mysteriously missing in the night?" Jessamine said.

"I thought maybe you'd think it was mice," Moss said.

"If Nonna had mice, they'd be so well fed there'd be no room leftover for cannoli," Joe said.

"Those would be some fat mice," Benny agreed.

The doorknob to their grandmother's room turned, and everyone lay down and closed their eyes. "Quick, shh," Moss said and promptly faked snoring. Their grandmother walked into the living room and paced back and forth beside their heads a few times, inspecting them for noise or trouble, the sound of her fluffy slippers squishing gently on the carpet. Satisfied that all was now quiet, she returned to her room and closed the door.

Milo's eyes popped open. He saw Jessamine staring at him, smiling.

"*Terrifying*," he mouthed.

She nodded and mouthed, *"Good night."*

He shifted closer and pressed a soft kiss to her lips. "Good night kisses at your grandmother's house don't count," he whispered in her ear.

"In that case," she whispered, pulling him closer for another kiss.

"If she comes back out, I'm throwing you two under the bus," Moss warned.

Jessamine let Milo go, but she didn't move away. They fell asleep, face-to-face, hands clasped between them. In the morning when Milo woke, he was alone on the floor.

"Is he sick?" he heard Jessamine's grandmother whisper.

"He doesn't like mornings, Nonna," Jessamine explained, also in a whisper.

"What's not to like about mornings?" Nonna asked.

"Everything, especially this early in the morning," Moss replied.

"You'd think having a baby would have made you a morning person by now," Joe replied.

"You'd think so, but you'd be wrong," Moss replied, yawning.

Milo was about to open his eyes and stand up when Nonna asked a question and the topic once again returned to him. "Explain to me again why he's here."

"Because someone has been trying to frighten me, and Milo is for protection," Jessamine replied.

"What does he do when he's not protecting you?" Nonna asked.

"He was a marine," Jessamine said.

"And what now?" Nonna asked.

"Nonna, he's protecting Jess now. That's enough," Joe said.

Nonna made a disgruntled clicking sound. "This is the first man she ever brings here, and I can't ask questions?"

"It's not like that, Nonna," Jessamine said.

"It's totally like that, Jess," Joe said.

"No, it's not. We've made it clear we're not together," Jessamine said.

"You've made it clear you're delusional," Moss said. "Denial isn't just a river in the Amazon."

"It's not a river in the...stop making geological references," Giovanni demanded, exasperated. To Jessamine he added, "What have we ever done to you to scare you off men so bad?"

"That's a valid question," Benny agreed.

They seemed to be waiting for an actual answer. "I'm not...cut out to be in that type of relationship," Jess stammered.

"Why not?" Joe demanded.

"Joe, come on," Jessamine said.

"Come on what, Jess? What do you think is so hard about being in a committed relationship? All of us are doing it," Moss said.

"Yes, well, all of you aren't me," Jessamine said. "I can't even believe we're having this discussion. You guys are the ones always telling me how controlling I am, how bossy."

"Jess," Giovanni breathed, sounding pained.

"You think you are the first bossy woman on the planet, eh? The other women in this family have faired very well in marriage, thank you very much," Nonna sniffed.

"It's not exactly the same," Jessamine said, trying to be delicate. "It's not like marrying Poppa took you away from a job you loved."

"Oh, is that it, you think you're so much better because you have a bigtime, important job," Nonna said, snorting. "Job, no job, marriage is about giving of yourself to someone else."

"I don't want to talk about this anymore. I'm going to shower," Jessamine said before going into the bathroom and closing the door.

"You can stop pretending to sleep now," Moss said, toeing Milo on the leg.

Milo sat up. "That didn't go well."

"Does anything with Jess go well?" Moss asked.

"Yes," Milo said, his gaze turning ponderously to the closed bathroom door. At his house, with him and Iz, Jessamine had let them in. She had relaxed and started to lower her guard. But now, back in the real world, her defenses were firmly in place. How did he get her to relent, to trust that he meant it when he said he wanted to be with her no matter what?

Giovanni sat down beside him. "When Viv and I were first

married, Jess found out. We were keeping it secret at the time, and Jess kind of flipped out, came up with this big, crazy scheme to get me to come around and reveal our secret. It didn't make much sense at the time, but now I'm wondering if it was a clue, if maybe it's what she needs, you know? Something to shake her out of the status quo."

Milo considered that. Being stalked had made her give in and allow him to guard her. Being attacked had made her give in and allow him to take her to his house. What would it take to make her give in and allow him to love her?

"Something to consider," he said with a grateful nod toward Giovanni.

The show in New York was a far cry from the one in Lexington. Filming in Lexington had been mildly exciting, but the size of the studio rivaled a small house. The studio in New York was massive, on the twenty seventh floor of a thirty-floor building. Milo felt a swoon coming on as soon as they entered the elevator. Jessamine, taking pity on him, slid her arm around him and kept it there the remainder of the ride.

"Okay?" she asked when they arrived on the correct floor.

"How hard are you trying to suppress your laughter right now?" he asked.

"The only thing holding it back is the desire not to ruin my mascara," Jessamine confessed. She took his hand and gave it a reassuring squeeze.

Milo sucked oxygen through his nose, breathing deep. He had to get it together; it wouldn't do for her security person to turn white and keel over at the sight of an elevator. As long as he avoided any windows, he could forget how high up they were. And, lucky for him, the studio had no windows. His heart rate began to come out of the stratosphere as soon as they emerged from the elevator. He gave Jess's hand a squeeze to let her know he was okay, but he didn't release it, even as he scanned the room, assessing for threats.

He felt anxious, and he wasn't certain if it was because of the height or something more sinister. His senses felt on high alert, as they often did when he had been on an assignment that was about to explode into something critical. The studio had its own security, as did the building. Their ID's had been checked on arrival. But it wasn't foolproof. Milo kept coming back to the memory of the police station. If the stalker could get to Jessamine there, he could get to her anywhere. Her appearance on the show had been pre-scheduled. And it marked the first time in two weeks she'd emerged from hiding. If he was intent on getting to her, now would be the perfect time—away from the security of home, in a massive city where disappearing was easy.

They were ushered into a green room. No one objected to Milo's presence or even seemed to notice him as the five Samperis were put into chairs, their hair and makeup prepped. The brothers, minus Moss, were clearly uncomfortable with the process. While they squirmed, looking as if they'd rather be anywhere else, he began a conversation with the stylist about the best product for maintaining his curls.

Milo tuned them out and focused on Jess. Her eyes found his in the mirror and they shared a smile. She was so incredibly stunning. How could they possibly enhance perfection? She didn't like it when he told her how beautiful she was, so he tried to say it with his eyes. When her cheeks flushed, he thought maybe he succeeded.

The stylists finished their work on the family. The brothers commenced teasing Moss about the girly curl products the stylist had given him. Jess eased from her chair and sat on the couch beside Milo. His arm slid around her, and she snugged closer, resting her head on his shoulder. It had become their standard position each night after they tucked Iz in. They sat together on the couch while Milo read out loud, until they were too tired to carry on, his free hand gently sifting her hair or gliding along her shoulder.

"What are you thinking about, looking so serious over here?" she asked.

"Lots of things. I'm, like, super deep and stuff," he said.

"Care to enlighten me?"

"No."

"Why?"

"Because you're about to go on TV, and I don't want to burden you." His finger skimmed her nose, and he smiled when she made a conscious effort not to wrinkle it or push him away. Of all the things they might have argued about, her nose had been the main source of contention lately.

It's my favorite feature, he'd told her.

That's not possible, you must be lying, Jessamine's reply had been terse, to say the least.

Okay, I'm lying. It's your lips. But this is a close second, he'd said, and then he touched it. She had pushed his hand away. Irritated by whatever made her see herself so unclearly, he'd kissed her senseless, only stopping when Iz arrived home from school and interrupted them.

Now he leaned closer and whispered in her ear. "I love your nose and there is absolutely nothing you can do about it."

"You're weird, but you're pretty, so I'll allow it," she said, sifting her fingers through his dark hair. "Fourteen year old me would have given anything to be here right now."

"How does thirty year old you feel about it?" he asked.

"She's a harder nut to crack."

"Tell me about it," he lamented.

"We're ready for you," one of the production assistants stepped inside, waiting to herd the Samperis on stage.

"Any last words of encouragement?" Jessamine asked.

"You're the most beautiful woman in the world, and I love you," Milo said.

"Well, that escalated quickly," Moss said, and then they were being whisked onstage while Milo remained off to the side, watching, scanning the studio for signs of a threat.

"Welcome, Samperis," the host, Madison Unger, said with a toothy grin. "Hosts of the wildly popular new renovation show that's taken America by storm. Or should I call you the yelling Samperis?"

"What?" Giovanni said, cupping his ear.

Madison laughed and turned her attention to Joe. "I have to tell you it feels like a bit of a coup to get you here, Joe. You're the reclusive Samperi."

"Joe's shy," Benny volunteered.

"He has to be because he's eight feet tall and five hundred pounds. If he's loud and outgoing people think he's a murderer," Moss added, and Madison laughed again.

"Jessamine, you've been filling the void as the family recluse lately. Care to tell everyone where you've been hiding?" Madison asked.

"I've been renovating a friend's house," Jessamine said.

"Lucky friend," Madison said. "Everyone's clamoring for your designs these days. You've been called the new Joanna Gaines."

"I would never presume to fill Joanna's shoes," Jessamine said. "Her designs are timeless, clean and classic."

"Moss, you're getting married soon, is that right?" Madison asked.

"Yes, and you're all invited," Moss tossed out to the crowd before slapping his hands over his mouth and shaking his head. "Never mind, forget I said that. My fiancée is going to kill me. Please don't show up at my house, we only have enough chicken for two hundred."

Madison laughed again. "It seems like you and Giovanni have some trouble getting along. Is that for the benefit of the cameras?"

"Yes," Moss said, while Giovanni said, "No."

"Oil and water, these two," Benny interjected.

"Benny, you and your wife recently returned from a honeymoon in Africa. That's an exotic destination," Madison said.

"It is. I'd been a few times before, and I wanted my wife to have the experience. We worked with a team digging wells and providing livestock as well as cooking stoves. You'd be surprised how many people still lack the basic necessities, even in our modern age. The charity is called Africanbasics.com, and they're always looking for generous donors or volunteers."

The remaining siblings exchanged smirks. Milo had heard them placing bets on how soon Benny would be able to broadcast a link to the charity.

"We'll be sure and put a link on our website," Madison promised him. It was prearranged, a condition of his appearance on the show, that they link to the charity, but he nodded, smiling, as if it was new information.

Madison lobbed a few more easy questions at the family, and they answered wittily, delighting the audience that had already been primed to adore them. Jessamine was a genuine celebrity now, and, if he were a different kind of man, it was the type of knowledge that could make Milo insecure. But he wasn't because, no matter how famous she became, she was still the same Jessamine, still the same woman with impossible barriers. *Those* were the real issue, not her adoring fans or overflowing talent or burgeoning bank account. None of that mattered if she wouldn't let him in.

"So," she said, pausing beside him when the segment was over.

"So," he said, smiling down at her but only slightly. She was tall, and he loved it. He loved everything about her, was crazy about her. At times when she pushed him away with both hands, he began to wonder if maybe he was just crazy.

"You think you're clever and cute, springing a bombshell declaration on me seconds before I go on live TV," she said, arms crossed over her chest.

"No, I think I'm sincere, and it's the same thing I've been telling you in a million different ways. Saying the words doesn't add much."

"It's been two months, Milo. Two months of ups and downs and a few dances and kisses, with no real dates to speak of."

"I could point out here that we've spent the last two weeks together 24/7. That we've seen each other in every possible scenario, most notably at our worst, that we understand each other's worst habits and are willing to overlook them. But what I'll say instead is that I knew the instant I walked in and saw you sitting on that bar stool. If you'd asked me before I met you if I believed in love at first sight, I would have said no. After my last horrendous decade-long relationship, I probably would have laughed and then run away screaming. I can't tell you how or why I knew in that instant you were the woman for me, but I know that I did. And I know the time we've spent together the last couple of months has only enhanced that knowledge. So there you go. Ball's in your court."

She gazed around the studio, most likely searching for a rescue. Finding none, she blew out a breath. "I'm starving. Want to grab something to eat? I know a great place."

"Is this deflection or denial?" he asked.

"Both," she said, but then she stood on her toes and kissed him lightly.

"You're good, but I'm persistent," he said.

"I know you are. It's why I require sustenance to deal with you," she said. She linked her arm with his and began leading him toward the exit.

They had a few hours to kill until their flight back home. Milo felt a strange mixture of elation and desperation. This was it—his last chance to make an impression. After this she would return to the real world and regular work. True, he would still be lingering in the background for a while, providing security. But it wouldn't be the same. She would be back to her job, back to her phone, back to her family and friends. For the last two weeks there had only been Milo and Iz in her view, and it had been his own private utopia. Now that he would once again have to share her with the masses, and most notably her job, it felt like the end. For the remainder of their time in New York, he vowed not to hound her. They would have a pleasant day together, some might call it an actual date, and then he would back off and leave it to her.

They exited the dim inner sanctum of the studio, blinking at the sudden harshness of the fluorescently lit outer shell.

"The elevators," Milo muttered. He had almost forgotten his dread.

"We're going down, it will be over soon," Jessamine said, patting his arm.

"See, I know you mean that to be comforting, but my brain hears that we're going to plummet and die."

"Do you know what I do when I'm this afraid of something?" Jessamine asked.

"What?" Milo asked.

"I don't know. I don't think I've ever been this afraid of something," she said, smiling up at him with mock innocence.

"Shame, Miss Samperi, shame. Mocking a soldier for his..." his phone buzzed with a text from Amara. His sister was keeping watch of Iz for him, and she wasn't the type to text in the middle of the day unless there was a problem. He withdrew his phone, hoping against hope that Iz wasn't sick. The flu was just beginning to make its rounds back home. He stared at his phone, his mind going blank with shock and panic at the words.

Iz is missing; I think she's been kidnapped.

*H*is brain blanked with horror, immediately imagining the worst-case scenarios. After working in intelligence for so many years, his mind conjured all of them. Then, slowly, reason began to return. Amara would never text that sort of information. She would call. His mother would call. The school would call. His other sisters would call. Probably even the police department would call, especially after he'd formed a working relationship with them. Something was wrong; something was off.

He turned to Jess, to run it by her, realizing as he did so that she was strangely silent in the face of his terror. And then the bottom dropped out of his world all over again; Jessamine was gone.

This time when his mind tried to short circuit with terror, he refused to let it, calling instead upon his training. First thing first, he needed help. He pulled up the numbers he'd programed, for both the building's security and that of the studio, and let them know what was going on. They would call the police while he began his search for Jess. He had previously familiarized himself with the building's layout, specifically this floor, so he knew he was standing beside the only elevator access. They would have to take the stairs. He headed in that direction at a sprint, hoping and praying he was right, that the psycho hadn't herded her into some abandoned office or something even more nefarious that he was overlooking. Instinct told Milo he would be looking for the quickest, easiest getaway. That meant the stairs.

They couldn't be that far ahead of him. He should see them, if he was on the right track. He was about to pivot away and search somewhere else when he rounded the corner and saw two forms dash into the stairwell. Jessamine was being herded, a gun shoved in her side. Her stalker wore a baseball cap, his form not anyone Milo immediately recognized.

"Stop," he called, letting them know he was close behind. He burst through the stairwell door, panting, and was faced with a new dilemma. Up or down?

"Up," Jessamine's voice echoed ghostlike from above. He dashed toward it, calling the building's security on his way.

He burst onto the roof, icy prickles of cold smacking him hard in the face. It was much colder in New York than back home in Kentucky. The sting was like an added jolt of mental clarity. Why the roof? There was nowhere to go but down from here, and there was only one way to do that. Surely he hadn't kidnapped Jessamine only to jump with her, had he?

"Milo," she called, her voice somewhere to his left. He dashed there now and saw his worst fear come to life. Jessamine and the guy perched on the ledge and let go, sliding easily over the side.

He opened his mouth—to scream?—but no sound came out. He both didn't want to see and yet had to, so his feet propelled him forward. But as he leaned over the side, he saw a window washer's scaffolding below him, the window beside it propped open. Jessamine and her stalker were on the platform, and now they were wrestling. The fall onto the platform must have jostled the gun out of his hand, or maybe Jessamine had gotten it away. Whatever happened, Jessamine was losing and in desperate need of assistance. Milo holstered his own gun, vaulted the edge of the building, and landed hard on the platform below. Picking up Jessamine as if she weighed nothing, he shoved her behind him and entered the fray.

He and the guy were evenly matched in size. His face was familiar, but Milo's brain was too focused to remember why. It was obvious the man had had some training and knew how to fight, but Milo had more. After a couple of rounds of intense back and forth, he was subdued, Milo's fist slammed into him a few more times, making sure he was good and unconscious.

The building's security guy arrived a minute later, followed by the police. At first they stood on the roof, peering down but, with no present emergency, descended to the floor below and leaned out the window, collecting the prisoner.

"I know him," Jessamine said. "He's a cop."

Milo recognized him, too, a newbie cop on their hometown force. It explained how he had accessed Jessamine at the police station—because he was already there—as well as how he tapped private information on her whereabouts that only cops had access to.

"Huh," Jessamine said, staring at the man as the NYPD did their thing. "So weird." She turned to face Milo and found him backed up against the edge of the scaffolding, frozen with terror, his face white. "Don't pass out." If he went unconscious, there was a good chance he would fall off the scaffold.

"Trying," he managed to say through rubbery lips. The sight of her was fading in and out. His heart felt as if it were trying to escape through his ribcage. He hadn't felt the usual terror when Jessamine had been in danger, hadn't given a thought to jumping from the roof to the platform below. But now that it was over...his ears began to ring, the telltale sign he was about to black out.

Jessamine strode forward and put her arms around him, standing on her toes to press her lips to his. "Stay with me," she murmured, kissing him.

Unbelievably, or maybe not so unbelievably, it worked. The icy terror began to leach away, replaced by an oozing warmth and comfort. "Walk this way," Jessamine whispered, keeping her lips on his as she led him in baby steps toward the window. Milo was shaking like a newborn lamb. His hands clutched her waist, his eyes clenched tightly closed. A stiff breeze rattled by him, and it was almost his undoing, but Jessamine cinched her arms around him, pressing their bodies tightly together. "Almost there," she murmured, and then four strong hands were pulling him inside. Finally, on solid ground, Milo gave in to the fear and everything went dark.

e had no idea how long he was out, nor what happened to him when he was unconscious. All he knew was that when he came to, he had come to some kind of resolution. Things with Jessamine weren't working as they should. Her stalker had been caught, and she had no more need of his services. He didn't delude himself they would continue on some kind of path. Even unconscious he could almost feel her straining at the bit to immerse herself in her world and in her work again. She would have no time for him, no place for him. Forgetting him would be all too easy. He wouldn't, couldn't stand by and let it happen.

His eyes popped open.

"Hey," Jessamine said. She sat on the floor, smiling down at him.

"Hey." He struggled to sit up. Around him, officers swirled with the busyness and efficiency of tying up loose ends. Jessamine's stalker was across the room in handcuffs, a cop either reading him his rights or asking him questions. "So I guess being in the NYPD is out for me."

Jessamine laughed and reached out to smooth her hand over his hair. "They were impressed that you leapt over the ledge, given your crippling anxiety and all. Are you doing okay? Do you want to go to the hospital?"

"No," he said, shaking his head hard. "I want to return to a place where there are no more than two floors in the entire town." He rubbed a hand over his face, feeling suddenly exhausted.

"I guess it's over," Jessamine said. She motioned to the stalker who was staring creepily at her, despite the room full of officers.

"Looks like," Milo agreed. He had the sense she was waiting for him to say something, to ask her to be with him so she could tell him no and move on. But he wouldn't. His unconscious brain had summoned what his wakeful self was unwilling to admit: she didn't want to be with him. "I have a job interview," he blurted instead.

"You do?" she asked, surprised. "That's great. What is it?"

"I can't exactly tell you because it's classified. But I'd be doing basically the same thing I did in the military, but as a civilian. It's in DC. Of course I have to actually get the job first, but I know the guy who's hiring, a former SEAL I worked with a couple of times. I can't say for certain, but I have the feeling the job is mine, if I want it."

"So you'd…you would have to relocate to DC," she said slowly.

"That's not ideal, obviously, but there's nothing here for me." His glance darted to her to make sure he hadn't wounded her. He hadn't. "Jobwise, I mean. There's still my family, but a guy has to support his kid somehow." He frowned, thinking of Iz. He would hate uprooting her again. But what was he supposed to do? How long could he reasonably go on being useless? Living on the last fading fumes of his savings account? He still owed Jessamine a thousand dollars for his car, a fact that weighed on him heavily.

"You're good at security," Jessamine conceded. She wrapped her arms around her legs and rested her head on them. "Sounds like maybe this will be the right fit for you."

Milo nodded, trying and failing not to be hurt by her lack of reaction. She had never promised him more. In fact, she had told him in every possible way that she wasn't interested. It was time he listened, time to set fantasy aside. He checked his watch. "By the time we're done here, I think we're going to have to go straight to the airport."

"You're probably right. It's a shame, I had a fun day planned for you." She smiled sweetly at him, and his heart turned over. Why couldn't she love him the way she should? On the other hand, he felt like he would be free in DC, free to focus on his job and Iz with no desire for anything else. He understood somehow that he would never get over her and move on, and maybe that was okay. Maybe it was even a blessing. His last relationship had hung on him like an albatross, distracting him in the field, weighing him with worry at all hours of the day and night. With Jessamine in possession of his heart, his mind would be free to focus on other things. Like a robot—all work, no pesky feelings to mess things up.

"You doing okay, bub?" A young officer knelt beside Milo, but his eyes were on Jessamine, his face alight with a flirtatious smile. Jessamine eased closer to Milo and rested her hand on his leg, dashing the officer's hopes. At least it was some comfort that, though she might not want Milo, she didn't want anyone else either.

"I'm doing fine," Milo said and tried to mean it. They were ending on a good note, as friends. And he still had his daughter, his family. Hopefully soon he'd once again have a career. All in all, it wasn't a bad life.

They gave their statements to the officers and a driver took them to the airport. The atmosphere between them was quiet, subdued. Possibly from exhaustion on Jessamine's part, but Milo knew better. For him it felt like saying goodbye to everything important, putting away his dreams for the future. He would find a new dream and a new life and try to forget that, for a minute, he had glimpsed perfection with her.

Jessamine slipped her hand into his and gave him a smile. "Thank you."

"You're welcome," he said, returning her smile.

"The last few weeks have been…nice. Is that a stupid thing to say when I've been in danger? Probably, but I really enjoyed getting to know you and Iz."

"Ditto," he agreed, squeezing her hand.

She turned her face to the window, and it was the last word they spoke until they said a stiff, formal goodbye at the airport.

CHAPTER 28

Moss's wedding day was beautiful. Bright, sunny, warm, and filled with chirping birds. It was exactly like what Moss would be like if he were a day. The fact that they had come so close to losing Molly only added to the specialness of the day and the joyous atmosphere.

There were three groomsmen—Joe, Benny, and Giovanni. Lou was the maid of honor, while Peaches and Jessamine were bridesmaids. Vivian, while not technically a bridesmaid, functioned as the surrogate flower girl, carrying Bella down the aisle, helping her pudgy baby fists toss a couple of handfuls of rose petals, and holding her up front through the ceremony.

Jessamine promised herself she wouldn't cry, but it was impossible not to with all of her brothers, both of her parents, and practically everyone else weeping. All any of them had to do was remember their terror on the night Molly was stabbed and the blubbering started all over again. Moss was a mess, a shameless spectacle of wet cheeks. Holding on to Bella seemed to be the only thing that could stem his tears, so he spent much of the day carrying her around.

"How many are you up to?" Peaches sidled close to Jessamine and whispered the question.

"Six, no seven," Jessamine said. Seven people so far had elbowed her and laughingly asked, *When's it going to be your turn?* "What about you?" How many people had asked her sweet sister-in-law when she was finally going to have a baby?

"Only three. I think word's getting around. Maybe your mom or dad said something," Peaches said.

"Probably Benny." Her older brother had a way of making people behave without actually calling out their gauche behavior. It was likely he had located the people most likely to ask Joe and Peaches intrusive questions on the state of their fertility and gently urged them not to. "Are you guys going to dance?" Joe was across the room, eyeing them sadly. The distance between the two was palpable, and Jessamine found it acutely painful. She wished she could fix it.

"At some point probably," Peaches said, sounding as sad as Joe looked. Jessamine hugged her, and Peaches returned it. "What about you? Are you going to snag a cousin and take a turn on the floor? I know how much you love to dance."

"I do love to dance," Jessamine agreed. She didn't want to dance with a cousin, though. She wanted to dance with…

"What?" Peaches asked tipping her face up to see why Jessamine had drawn in such a sharp breath.

"I'll be back in a minute," Jessamine said, easing away. The wedding was being held at her parents' house. She headed for the long drive-way, ignoring anyone who tried to talk to her. She found her car, maneuvered out of the makeshift parking lot, and drove at maximum speed toward Milo's house. Would he be there? Was he already in DC?

He stood curiously on the porch when she arrived, shading his eyes to see who would visit unannounced in the middle of the after-noon on a Saturday, likely believing it was one of his sisters.

When he realized it was her, she watched his expression shift from curious to wary and felt a pang that he had reason to be self-protec-tive. She had hurt him, even without meaning to, she had hurt him.

"Hey," he said, "aren't you supposed to be in a wedding?"

"I'm heading back in a minute, but it occurred to me I don't know how your interview turned out," she said. Her hands clutched together behind her back, her nails digging into the opposing palm until it became painful. She focused on the pain to keep her voice and face neutral.

"They offered me the job. Ten thousand more than I made in the marines, plus moving expenses. My mom offered to come with me to keep an eye on Iz. Lots of travel."

"Oh," Jessamine said. "When do you go?"

"I don't." His hands eased into his pockets, his face and voice impassive.

"What?"

"I turned them down, I didn't take the job."

Her heart started to flutter. "Why not?"

He swallowed hard and looked away. "I got out of the marines to be a fulltime dad. Undoing that would be only for my wounded pride. It's best for Iz if I stay here and be a parent. I lost sight of that for a moment, but no more. I got offered a job as the head of security at a hospital in Lexington. The pay is lousy, but it's stable with good hours. I'll be able to be present for all the moments."

"Is that the only reason you stayed? For Iz?"

He sighed and crossed his arms over his chest. "What do you want me to say here, Jess? Do you want me to beg?"

"Kind of," she said.

He blinked at her, the corner of his mouth lifting slightly. "Would it do any good?"

"I think so, but the words need to be specific," she said.

"Are you going to tell me what they should be? Because I feel like I've tried everything, and I don't know what to say anymore," he said.

She unclasped her hands and took a step forward, her fingers twisting nervously together in front of her now. "I want you to tell me again the good parts of marriage and parenthood because I haven't been able to get them off my mind since last time. When you talked about whispering together in the night, feeding a baby milk from my body, a baby made in a mad rush of love, my mind keeps playing that over and over again, and it's always our baby, yours and mine. And Iz is there, smiling in the background, a proud big sister." She took another step forward. "And we live here, but of course I've made it better, followed through on the renovations in my head. We'll need a few more bedrooms and bathrooms, a new kitchen for certain. The barn is perfect but in need of horses."

He came down off the porch and stood in front of her, close but not touching. "What changed your mind?"

"The lack of you," she said, easing her arms around him and pressing against him, her softness to his strength.

His hands rested on her hips, and he smiled. "All I had to do to get you was go away and let you be the one in pursuit?"

"I think I might be the man in this relationship," she whispered.

"I think you might be right, and I am one hundred percent okay with that." He kissed her and she returned it, standing on her toes to melt into him. For the first time she let go completely, and it felt so good to hold nothing in reserve, to give him everything and trust him to take care of it.

"Hey, what's going on?" Iz said. She stood on the porch eyeing them with the same wary expression Milo had worn. "You guys are kissing."

"Yes," Milo said.

"Are you going to get married?" Iz asked, a sad amount of suppressed hopefulness in her tone.

"Eventually," Milo said, clasping Jessamine's hand.

"How would you both like to go to a wedding? I need a dance partner and, Iz, you need to meet your future family."

"Really?" Iz said, excited. Jessamine nodded, and she scurried off, presumably to get changed.

"How long do you think we have before she comes back?" Milo asked, reaching for her again.

"Not nearly long enough. And you need to get changed, too. I plan to parade you vindictively in front of a lot of people, seven specifically."

"Okay, but I have to tell you something before we go. Don't be mad."

She frowned slightly. "I'm listening."

"I forgot to check the garbage disposal before I turned it on. Let's just say we're probably going to need a new one, plus possibly some new forks and a lid for the olive oil."

"No problem," Jessamine assured him.

"Also, I broke the window in the kitchen."

"I'm planning to do away with that wall anyway," she said.

"And somehow I cracked a tile in the…"

She pressed her palm to his mouth. "Milo, did you do these things to, on some subconscious level, get me to come back and fix them?"

"Sure, let's go with that," he said, smiling.

"I'll make a deal with you. I will keep the house in good running repair if you do the same for my heart. I'm going to struggle to find balance between work and family. I'm going to try and push you aside. Don't let me."

"I'm fairly good at dogged determination," he said.

"It's one of my favorite things about you," she said.

"I'd like to hear the others," he whispered, leaning in to skim her lips.

"Well, first there's your…"

"Ready," Iz declared, stepping back onto the porch.

Milo gave Jessamine a squeeze and let her go. "I guess that's my cue to go change."

"Iz, let me do your hair while he's doing that," Jessamine said. She ascended the porch and put her arm around Iz to shepherd her to the bathroom. Milo held the door for them and followed them inside, content with the knowledge that he'd be doing so for many years to come.

*T*hank you for reading *A Total Teardown*, The Builders series book four. For more books, please visit my website at www.vanessagraybartal.com